REACHING THE HEIGHTS

PETER GUNNING

BLACKWATER PRESS

For Finbarr and Sinéad

Age group 10 – 14 years

First published in 1995
by Blackwater Press,
Hibernian Industrial Estate, Greenhills Road,
Tallaght,
Dublin 24

Produced in Ireland by Folens Publishers.

Editor: Deirdre Whelan
Assistant Editor: Zoë O' Connor
Design: Philip Ryan

ISBN: 0 86121 810 8 1334
British Library Cataloguing-in-Publication Data.
A catalogue record for this book is available farm the British Library.
Gunning, Peter. Reaching the Heights.

Contents

Chapter 1
The Match

"For God's sake, Naylor, hurry on! The bus will be gone!" called Tosh in an annoyed voice. Naylor was never ready on time.

"I can't find me stockings. Me mam washed them and I don't know where she put them!" Naylor was frantically rummaging through the hot press searching for his football socks.

"Well I'm not waiting any longer! I'm off!" Tosh turned on his heels and headed for the lift.

"Hang on!" roared Naylor. "I found them!" He ran out the door, busily stuffing the socks into his gear bag as he joined his friend at the lift.

"Damn thing is out of order again!" grumbled Tosh.

"Come on, Tosh! We'll use the stairs!"

The two ran niftily down the four flights jumping three steps at a time and rounding each corner with youthful abandon. Once out of the building they galloped in the direction of the bridge where the bus was preparing to pull away.

Gary was mad with them. He stood there with his notebook and pen and gave them that "one more minute and we were gone without you" stare.

"It was his fault!" claimed Tosh. "Too busy looking through his mother's underwear!"

"Watch it!" threatened Naylor.

"Get on that bus before I kick your backsides! The pair of you should be left on the line for giving me near heart failure!" Gary shook his head. With him you never knew whether he was serious or not.

Gary Quigley had been their manager for the past three years, ever since he moved to Cork. In his late twenties he was tall and well built and had played inter-county football for Wexford before a serious knee injury put an end to his promising playing career. None of the lads knew much about him, apart from the fact that he owned a local bakery and lived in an apartment near the city centre.

Once on the bus the breathless pair sat in silence. It was only a league game against Bishopstown but they would be meeting the same side in the championship final in three weeks time. Gary reckoned that it would be a good dress rehearsal for the big day.

Tosh loved football. Nothing gave him more pleasure than lining out with the Heights in his number nine jersey. Centre field! He especially loved dry sunny days when the ball would bounce and move more quickly. Tall for his age and with good hands, he loved to rise above his opponents and cleanly field those high balls.

Naylor was different. He wasn't really very good. He didn't particularly like playing football at all. He was small and skinny and without his glasses he could see very little. Once he was playing in a hurling match and was marking a much taller boy. All of a sudden a crow flew overhead. Thinking it to be the ball, Naylor took a wild swing at the bird! Obviously he missed but the hurley clattered down on the head of his opponent. He was sent off. Too embarrassed to explain to the referee about his poor eyesight, he was suspended for two months for violent conduct! He gave up hurling after that, although Tosh managed to persuade him to keep up the gaelic football. At least he could see the ball... just about!

As the bus weaved its way through the Cork city streets, Naylor's mind wasn't on the battle with Bishopstown which lay ahead. His mother hadn't been well. She hadn't said anything but he could tell. Sometimes he would notice it in her voice or in the way she would walk. This time he could see it in her face. Her eyes looked so tired and her cheeks were pale and drawn. Something was really troubling her. Naylor worried about his mother. Last month he overheard a loan shark threatening her. He didn't sleep for a week. Naylor was that sort of kid. At thirteen years of age he carried in his mind the anxieties and concerns of an adult.

Not that Naylor's situation was unusual. Every kid living in McGillicuddy Heights had a similar story to tell. It was a tough area. Unemployment was widespread. Crime, particularly juvenile crime, was a serious problem. So too were drugs. Loan sharks and pushers preyed on the residents turning the Heights into a beehive of despair. Kids stole to buy dope. Mothers borrowed to buy bread. It was a no win situation for those who lived there.

"Tosh, you're centre-field again today. Take the number nine shirt. Naylor we'll give you a chance at corner back." Gary dished out the shirts as he informed his charges of their positions.

"Great stuff!" said Tosh as he relished the prospect of his central role.

"Corner back!" groaned Naylor. "I'll be bloody well murdered! Come on, Gary! Let me play in the forwards!"

"Sorry, Naylor! No can do!" replied Gary as he moved on up the bus with his arms full of the numbered shirts.

"You'll be fine, Naylor. Just stick close to your man and keep your eyes on the ball!"

"Easier said than done!" replied his bespectacled friend as he made a mental note to check out the possibility of obtaining contact lenses with his medical card.

Chapter 2
The Letter

Aisling read the letter over and over again. She couldn't believe her eyes. Her hand trembled. She felt weak. Still trying to come to terms with its contents, she moved to the couch and sat down. This time she took a deep breath and decided to read it again, slowly and carefully. How could she...? She shook her head. Her own mother! How could she...?

She stuffed the letter awkwardly into its envelope and put it back on the kitchen table alongside the one addressed to her father. God knows when he would get around to reading his. He hadn't come home last night. That was no surprise. He was becoming quite an expert at not finding his way home. Home? She thought about the word. Such a miserable little word.

She sat on a high stool at the breakfast bar and buried her head in her hands. She was trembling again. She had to do something. She couldn't just sit around all day. The house was big and empty. She missed the usual Saturday post-lunch noise as her brothers, Finbarr and Aengus, would grapple for possession of the TV remote.

Finbarr was a twelve-year-old sports fanatic, while ten-year-old Aengus would live on a diet of MTV.

The silence made her shiver. She put on her ski jacket and wrapped her long black woollen scarf around her neck. She switched on the alarm and slammed the front door closed as she left. The gravel underfoot crunched as she made her way to the shed. There she found her bike sandwiched between the mountain bikes belonging to her brothers. As she prised her own free she felt overwhelmingly lonely.

Putting on her walkman she turned the volume up fully. She cycled away from the house with U2's "I Still Haven't Found What I'm Looking For" belting her eardrums.

Aisling cycled aimlessly for two hours. When she left her home in Douglas she found herself heading along the scenic byroads which led to the coast. The cold sea breeze gradually became more prevalent and coaxed Aisling to turn back. Soon she became aware of an increased presence of traffic as she joined the heavy city centre-bound flow. She stopped in Patrick Street and chained her bike to a railing near the taxi rank across from the Savoy. Saturday afternoon shoppers littered both sides of the street. Like swarming bees they hovered in and out of stores carrying assorted plastic bags. Aisling joined in the swarm moving in and out of the various shops. She turned off U2 for a while and the buzzing city sounds exploded in her ears. She wandered into a boutique and started to browse while all the time her thoughts raced wildly.

"Can I help you?" The store manager's voice was not friendly.

"Pardon?"

"Can I help you?" he repeated even more sternly than before with his angry eyes fixed on the sweater Aisling had been trying on for the past fifteen minutes.

"Oh... you mean this!" exclaimed Aisling, suddenly realising why this man in the dark grey suit was talking to her, "No... I mean, I don't think it suits me... I'll just put it back."

Aisling returned the sweater to the shelf and hurried back to her bike. She had had enough of beeping car horns, exhaust fumes, crying babies and irritable boutique managers. However, she wasn't ready to return to the house. She cycled to the top of Patrick Street and turned left. Blarney sounded like a good idea. Pauline lived there. Maybe she could talk to her.

As it turned out talking to Pauline was not possible. Pauline wanted to do all the talking herself.

"Well I don't know how I kept a straight face! There I was talking to Eamonn when Brian came out of the pool hall." Pauline was on to her favourite subject again!

"So I said to Eamonn, 'Watch now and he'll come over!' And of course he did!"

"Pauline... " Aisling tried to change the subject but it was no use. Pauline was in full throttle.

"Bold as a brass monkey he asked me straight out was I finished with Stephen Kenny. Well myself and Eamonn just burst out laughing! I thought my two sides would split! Poor old Brian just stood there not knowing what was going on. For crying out loud, I mean at this stage of the game the guy should have been able to take a hint. I mean to say, did he not see Eamonn?"

"Pauline, I've got a problem!" Aisling again tried to win Pauline's attention.

"Haven't we all? I have three guys wanting to go out with me and I fancy a fourth! Still I'll stick with Eamonn for another week or two. He's kind of cute! He bought me a burger!"

"Really?" offered Aisling without enthusiasm.

"Yeah! A quarter pounder with cheese!"

"Pauline, do you want to listen to my problem or not?"

"Oh sure Aisling! But first I want to give Fiona a buzz and find out is she still interested in Kieran McMahon. He's a fine bit of gear!"

Pauline left the bedroom and picked up the phone in the hallway. Aisling soon heard the giggling and details of the same giddy story about Brian, Eamonn, Stephen and Kieran McMahon. She told her about the burger too! Aisling had had enough of Pauline for one day. It wasn't going to be possible to discuss her parents' marital problems with somebody who measures love on a scale from plain to quarter pounder with cheese. Pauline was a silly empty-headed fourteen-year-old without a care in the world. Wasn't she the lucky one, thought Aisling.

"Are you off?" asked Pauline, somewhat surprised as she momentarily put down the receiver.

"Yeah... got to go! See you on Monday!" came Aisling's reply as she pulled the door behind her.

She cycled hard back in towards the city. As she approached the outskirts, McGillicuddy Heights came into view. The grey rectangular blocks cut bluntly into the

February skyline. Aisling thought of Tosh and Naylor. She liked them both. Especially Tosh. He was handsome and intelligent and yet so unassuming. He was shy too which is what Aisling found so appealing. The other girls in school would go on about his good looks or his brilliance on the sports field. However, to Aisling, it was this quiet, shy quality which she found so attractive.

She liked Naylor too but in a more sisterly sort of way. It used to annoy her when some of the guys at school teased him. He worked very hard, so much so that he fell into the unpopular swot category. The teasing never amounted to more than the odd jeer or silly joke. They called him "The Professor". Even though Naylor seemed to take it all in his stride there were times when Aisling noticed that he was hurt.

"Don't let them get to you, Tony!" she would tell him.

"It's okay for them!" he would say. "They don't have to do well here!"

Even though Aisling didn't entirely agree with him she understood what Naylor meant. She would just smile and tell him that if he ended up being a professor then he wouldn't be doing too badly then, would he?

Passing the Heights she was tempted to call in and look for Tosh or Naylor. She turned left at The Bowlers' Inn and headed down the narrow lane which led from the main in-bound city road to the Heights. However, ahead of her was a gang shouting and laughing. She braked. From where she looked they seemed to be having a cider party. Brown two litre bottles were being passed around a disorderly circle. A group of three or four crouched in a corner with their heads buried in white plastic bags. Sniffers, she guessed. In all there must have been about fifteen of them. Suddenly she heard a bottle breaking followed by more laughing. Different this time, though. Threatening, with a hint of violence. Not wishing to risk either a puncture or a mugging, Aisling decided against seeking out her friends. She turned her bike around and headed back towards the city centre. She would have to wait until Monday now.

Chapter 3
Short Cut

Tosh too heard breaking glass. He was coming home from the chipper with Naylor.

"Damn it, Tosh! Will we go back through the church instead?"

"I don't know. Who is it?"

"I'm not sure, I can't see properly. My glasses are loose again. It sounds like the O'Callaghan gang!"

Tosh peered down the lane.

"You're dead right, Naylor! And they're doing glue with cider!"

"Loony cocktails!"

Another cider bottle crashed to an aggressive roar of approval.

"Sod this, Tosh! They're as high as kites! I'm going back through the church.

"That makes two of us! I'm too young to be a martyr!"

The two turned away from the lane and walked briskly into Church Street. Tea-time traffic was heavy. As they ate their battered sausages and chips, car horns beeped impatiently and slow moving buses and lorries spluttered their filthy fumes into the misty early evening semi-darkness.

"I think I'll do that English essay on 'Pollution' tonight!" suggested Tosh.

"Frig all else to do tonight anyway!" added Naylor.

"I'll call mine 'A Walk on the Northside on a Saturday Evening'!"

"Very clever!"

"Hey!" shouted Tosh suddenly, almost choking on a chip. "There's Aisling O'Gorman!"

"Where?" Naylor was equally surprised.

"Behind the Smarties bus! Aisling! Aisling!"

They both started to call her but it was no use. Aisling had once again decided to listen to Bono and the boys on her long cycle home. As Tosh and Naylor frantically tried to attract her attention, U2 were telling her that they still hadn't found what they were looking for. She pulled out in front of the bus and began to weave her way through the lines of crawling vehicles until she was eventually out of sight.

"She's a fine thing, eh Tosh!" enthused Naylor.

"What would you know about it?"

"I dunno! I think she fancies me!"

"Get away!"

"She does, Tosh, honest! She is always very friendly. She says nice things to me!"

"Like what?"

"You know... nice things!"

"No, I don't know! What nice things?"

"Things like, 'How are you doing?'"

"'How are you doing?' Where's the big deal in that?"

"There isn't one. But it proves that she likes me. Which is more than can be said for that snobby shower that she hangs around with!"

"They can't help being snobby. That's the way they were born," suggested Tosh.

"Yeah! Rich and stupid!"

"Better than being poor and stupid!"

"We're not stupid, Tosh!" boasted Naylor in a proud voice he always used when he was getting serious.

"Maybe not! But we're frigging poor, though!"

They both laughed and sat on the steps outside the church where they finished off their chips. The early evening mass goers were beginning to filter in for the six o'clock. Tosh and Naylor shared a can of coke and proceeded to have a belching competition. A little old lady gave them a filthy look as she made her way past them into the church.

"You two ought to be ashamed of yourselves! Outside God's house and all!"

When she disappeared into the church they both exploded with laughter.

"I'm ashamed of myself!" chuckled Naylor, mimicking the old lady's haughty tones.

"Me too!" agreed Tosh and they both laughed again. However, deep down they did feel just a little bit guilty.

"Will we go in?" asked Naylor when they had recovered from the laughter.

"To mass?"

"Yeah."

"Might as well. It'll save me having to get up in the morning. The old fella is a stickler about mass."

"So is me mam. Come on so!"

"I'm gonna pray the old fella wins the Lotto tonight!" grinned Tosh as he got up stiffly form the cold concrete step.

"You never told me he could count to forty-two!"

"Get lost! The man's a genius."

They laughed again as they trampled across the car park. The crunching of the gravel underfoot seemed in tune with their chuckles. Once inside they marched up the centre aisle and sat to the right of the altar. Tosh wanted to sit down at the back but Naylor told him he could see damn all down there. Even though Tosh couldn't figure out just what exactly it was which Naylor wanted to see he didn't argue. They sat in silence. The light-heartedness of just a few moments ago was soon forgotten as they waited for the arrival of the priest.

Naylor was soon lost in deep thought about his mother. He liked being in church. He liked the empty silence broken occasionally by the echoing of high heels on marble or an infant crying in its mother's arms. Sounds made sense in a church. There was a feeling that things were normal. Candles flickered on the dimly-lit altar casting long shadows under the giant crucifix. Naylor's thoughts wandered with the shadows. For a while he felt safe. Even though he was at an age when he was easily embarrassed and possibly overly sensitive he knelt and buried his head in his hands. He prayed. He knew Tosh wouldn't tease him. Others might have called him a Holy Joe or a Mr Moses. But not Tosh. Tosh wouldn't say anything at all. Tosh understood.

The bell sounded for mass to begin and Naylor stood next to his friend. Neither spoke during the mass except at the collection time when Tosh threw the ring of the coke can into the plate and Naylor couldn't hold back the giggles.

Tosh day-dreamed all though the mass. Every time Fr O'Leary spoke his mind wandered. He thought of Aisling O' Gorman. What was she doing on the northside on a Saturday afternoon? Shouldn't she be horse-riding or pony-trekking or whatever else it is rich girls do at weekends? Why was she cycling through the Heights?

Tosh liked Aisling. From the outset she had been welcoming to both himself and Naylor. They were the only two kids from the Heights who were in Freemount Secondary. Most of the kids from their local primary school, St Peters, went straight into the adjacent secondary school. When they were in sixth class Mrs Baines advised them to have a go at the entrance examination for Freemount. It was a new multi-denominational school on the southside of Cork. Most of the others laughed.

"They wouldn't want us, Miss!"

"We'd have to do elocution to get in there, Miss!"

"That place is only for the hobnobs, Miss!"

Mrs Baines had other ideas.

"Entrance to Freemount is by open competition. The only person stopping you from going will be yourself!"

Tosh was tempted. It wasn't that there was anything wrong with the the Heights or the northside. It was just that he wanted to be a bit different, to go somewhere where he wasn't known. It seemed like a great idea to go to a school on the far side of town. The spin on the bus would be great crack alone!

Naylor wasn't easily convinced. The thought of travelling across town and mixing with all those rich kids. Snobby gits!

Besides, how could he afford the bus fare every day. It was out of the question.

But it wasn't! Tosh worked on him. Firstly he found out that they might be entitled to free bus passes. He also made him come to terms with the idea of mixing with the so called "snobby gits"!

"We're every bit as good as they are! We've every right to go to that school!"

In the end it was the exam results which made Naylor's mind up for him. They were both offered places a week after sitting the entrance test and interview.

"It was a breeze, Tosh! Once your man asked me about computers I was away with it!"

Naylor was a computer whiz-kid. They had three computers in St Peters and he persuaded Mrs Baines to allow him to spend every spare minute working on them. She was always giving him new software to try out and computer magazines to read. After his interview at Freemount he was shown the computer department.

"It was like something out of *Star Trek,* Tosh! They've got everything! If this bus pass thing doesn't work out then I'll flaming well walk!"

"Maybe you'll be beamed up each morning!" suggested Tosh.

The bus pass did work out though and Naylor's feet were spared the five mile north to south trek across the city. There were times in those first few weeks when they did feel a little out of place. Tosh remembered his first day in the school canteen. Two guys next to him were tucking into fresh seafood sandwiches. They were about three inches thick and packed with salmon, crabmeat and prawns. He felt a bit out of it as he sat there with his egg sandwich and packet of Chipsticks!

However, despite the odd moment of feeling empty of pocket, both he and Naylor settled in well to life at Freemount. Tosh played soccer, gaelic football and rugby for the school. Rugby was a totally new game to him. He had seen it on the telly when Ireland were playing but found it hard to follow all the rules. He still didn't fully understand them but it never seemed to matter. All he ever had to do was to run to the line with the ball or throw it back to a team-mate if tackled.

Naylor didn't bother with any sports teams. He learned how to play chess though and between that and his computer projects he never seemed to have any free time.

"Let us offer each other the sign of peace!" ordered Fr O'Leary gently from the altar. Tosh woke from his day-dream with a start and shook Naylor's extended hand. He didn't bother saying "Peace be with you" and neither did Naylor. They just nodded at each other. Tosh turned around to shake the hand of the person behind him. He hated doing this. It was always a bit embarrassing shaking hands and wishing strangers peace. His face dropped. He was offering his hand to the lady who had chastised them for the belching competition!

"Peace be with you," she offered in a friendly voice as she shook his hand.

Tosh smiled back.

"And with you," he replied. He felt better in himself. Maybe this part of the mass wasn't such a bad idea after all.

Soon people were shuffling up to communion. Naylor went but Tosh stayed where he was. He wanted to go back to his day-dream. He wanted to think about Aisling again.

A lovely thought struck him. Maybe she was looking for *him.* Why else would she be passing the Heights? Nobody in their right minds would go for a cycle around the Heights. It was the only place in Cork excluded from the annual Streets of Cork cycling race. That was after the year a German rider took a wrong turn and had his bike and cycling gear stripped from him. It was a tourist no-go area! So what in the name of God was Aisling doing there? She must have been looking for him. There was no other explanation. He sat back in his bench and grinned.

"What are you smirking at?" asked Naylor when he returned from communion.

Tosh smiled back at him.

"Don't worry, Naylor! You'll be the first to know!"

Chapter 4

Mother

Naylor immediately knew that there was something wrong. The glass panel had been smashed and the door itself had obviously been forced as it hung limply on one hinge.

Naylor's heartbeat raced as he entered the flat. His mouth went suddenly dry and a buzzing filled both ears. Inside there was silence.

"Mam!" he called nervously. "Where are you, Mam?"

The buzzing in his ears grew more intense as his nervousness gave way to terror. He saw that the kitchen door had been left ajar. That wasn't like his mam. She always closed doors behind her. He pushed in the door and found her there.

"Mam!" he screamed, "Jesus, Mam! What happened?"

She lay on her side on the kitchen floor. Though still conscious she was unable to speak. Her face and mouth were so badly swollen that her tongue was practically immobile. Congealed blood hung in tangled clots from her eyebrows. Her hair was similarly matted. He tried to lift her but her scream was so anguished he left her down again. He noticed both collar-bones were coming out at different angles under the bloodstained fabric of her dress.

"Mam! Mam! Who did this to you?" he stammered as he tried to take in what was going on. He felt as if he was floating in an unreal world.

She didn't answer. She just moaned. Her breathing was distressed and becoming overly pronounced. He had to get an ambulance. He had to get to a phone. Fast!

He banged his fist on the metal door of the lift. The vibrations echoed downwards to the ground four floors below. Out of order! Damn it! He cursed out loud. He threw himself down each flight and before he knew it he found himself in the laneway surrounded by the O'Callaghan gang. They were still entertaining friends over Evostick.

“Let me through! Me mam is in trouble! I’ve got to get to a phone!” he begged. It was no use. They weren’t on this world. Their brain cells were so far blown they weren’t in any position to exercise powers of reason.

“Sure God love us!” teased Mattie O’Callaghan. He was the youngest of them but one hundred per cent savage.

“Me poor mammy!” jeered Axle O’Callaghan. Another savage.

“Hey, is this young Naylor we have here?” spoke Sledge. The leader of the pack. Half ape half pre-ape!

“Let me go, Sledge! I have to get to a phone! Somebody beat up me mam!” Naylor was begging again.

“Money!” demanded Axle, sounding like Cookie Monster in Sesame Street.

“I don’t have any money!”

“Oh no?” It was Sledge again. He was moving closer in. This was getting serious.

“Not a penny! I swear to God!”

“Well I think I’ll take a closer look!”

Before he had a chance to look any closer Sledge found himself doubled up in a heap. Naylor’s knee arrived with tremendous force right between his legs. As Sledge rolled around in agony clutching himself, Naylor attempted to flee. Axle was the quickest of them to react. He grabbed Naylor by the throat and squeezed. Naylor felt the blood supply to his brain being cut off. All he could see was the evil in Axle’s eyes which began to disappear as his vision blurred. Axle tightened his grip and Naylor thought his head was going to explode. Just as he was on the point of collapse a mental picture of his mother lying on that kitchen floor flashed before his eyes. Axle suddenly drew back his head as he prepared to hammer it down on his choking victim. However, the thought of his mother awakened an inner strength in Naylor. As Axle’s head came up Naylor met it with an almighty head-butt. He caught Axle on the bridge of the nose. A sudden snapping noise was followed by a gush of blood. Axle staggered, releasing his grip, and Naylor sprinted out of the laneway. To his amazement he wasn't followed. He glanced back and saw Axle with his head buried in his hands, and Sledge rolling around and holding on for dear life.

The phone was working. He dialled 999 and waited.

"Ambulance, please, and Gardai to Flat 42 McGillicuddy Heights... My number?... I don't have one... This is a payphone... Mmm, it's hard to see... Someone has scratched it out... I think it says 343246... Look! What bloody difference does it make what number it is?... My mother is lying in a pool of blood so will you cut this bull and send an ambulance!... Okay! .... Yeah I know that... Yeah... I'm sorry, but could you please help me?... Yeah... My name is Tony O'Neill... Yes, my mother... Mrs Betty O'Neill... Flat 42 on the fourth floor... McGillicuddy Heights... Yeah, that's right... Thank you... Oh, by the way, Miss, would you ever ask the guards to pick me up outside the Credit Union... Well there's this gang hanging around Heights' Lane... No, I don't know who they are... Thanks very much, Miss... Thanks a lot."

The ambulance arrived with siren blaring and lights flashing within five minutes. Naylor sat in the squad car where a garda who asked him to call her Linda kept telling him not to worry.

"Everything is under control now, Tony." But Naylor wasn't so sure.

The ambulance crew carefully lifted Mrs O'Neill onto the stretcher. It all seemed very matter of fact. They put a mask to her face to help her to breathe and gave her a shot of something to ease her pain. Naylor was terrified. It was all too businesslike for his liking. That was his mother they were treating like just another number.

"Mind how you lift her!" he ordered. He felt a bit stupid saying that but thought he should not let the moment pass without commenting in some way.

"Don't worry, son! We won't hurt your mam," promised the older of the two ambulance men.

"It's okay, Tony, your mother is going to be just fine," ensured Linda.

"But she can hardly breathe! And all that blood everywhere!" Naylor was getting upset.

"Once they get her to hospital they'll make her more comfortable."

"Now then, Tony, where are you going to go tonight?" asked the other garda who introduced himself as Jack.

"How do you mean?" Naylor didn't understand.

"Well you can't stay here, that's for sure. Do you have an aunt or somebody we can drive you to?"

"Er... no."

"No relation?" Linda sounded surprised.

"Er, no. Nobody. Except for my nan. But she's senile and lives in a home outside Bandon. Not much point in bringing me there!"

There was an embarrassed pause.

"Do you know of any neighbour who might oblige... at least until Monday. By then we should know just how exactly your mother is and we might be able to make more satisfactory arrangements for your welfare."

"What do you mean 'more satisfactory arrangements'?"

"You're a juvenile Tony," explained Jack, "You can't possibly stay on your own and it would be unfair to expect a neighbour to take responsibility... "

"Tosh!" interrupted Naylor before Jack had a chance to explain the fostering procedure any further.

"Pardon?"

"I'll go to Tosh. He's me mate. Me best friend. He lives with his dad up on the fifth... Flat 55. His dad is sound. It's just the two of them there so there won't be a problem. Mr Twomey will understand. Sure he and my mam are great friends!"

"Fine! That sounds ideal... provided Mr Twomey agrees. Now where can we find them. The next floor up? Flat 55 you said, was it?"

Naylor suddenly remembered that Tosh's dad was never in

before eleven. He always went for a long walk every night and would stop off in The Bowlers' for a game of cards or darts on the way home. He had to think fast before he found himself the property of the Southern Health Board.

"Look! I'm going to the hospital with my mother. I want to make sure they give her a decent bed. I want to talk to the doctors. Find out what is really wrong with her. We can talk to Mr Twomey when you drive me home later."

"I don't know, Tony." Linda wasn't convinced. "There's very little point in your coming to the hospital... "

"She's me mam! If I don't go she'll have nobody!"

"But it might be all hours before we get back here. We couldn't be knocking up Mr Twomey then. It wouldn't be fair."

"I'm telling you he's dead sound! He wouldn't mind. He always stays up late reading. He never goes to bed before two or three in the morning. The man is an owl!"

There was another pause followed by a nodding of heads. Naylor had convinced them.

"Okay, Tony, you win! The two of us will ride in the ambulance with your mother and Jack will follow in the squad."

The ambulance was scary. A humid smell of disinfectant hung heavily. Tubes hung from the ceiling and there seemed no end to the machines going "bleep". The mask was taken from his mother's face and a new green one was placed on it. The nurse who travelled with the crew adjusted a dial overhead and a cloud of dust-like vapour buzzed as it worked its way up a tube and into the face mask.

"It's okay, Tony. It's only a nebulizer. We just have to give your mother a little help to breathe so we're giving her some oxygen."

She then began to clean the congealed blood away but her face looked no better. It was swollen and puffy and totally covered with red and purple blotches. It frightened him to see her lying there. Tubes and masks and smells of disinfectant. He was scared. He had never felt as alone as he did in the back of that ambulance. Ever since his father had walked out it had been just the two of them. That had happened years before when Naylor was still a baby. He had never remembered life any other way. His father was a photograph on the sideboard. His mother was his family. Now as she lay there on the stretcher bed his worst fears began to swell up inside him. A wave of terror washed through him. He reached over and took her hand. He squeezed her fingers tightly.

"Mam," he whispered softly. "It's me... Tony."

There was no response. He lifted her hand to his mouth and kissed her fingers.

"Mam... It's me, Tony... Don't leave me, Mam. Please don't leave me!" Slowly she raised her free hand and gently stroked his hair. Tears rolled down his cheeks as he met his mother's eyes. He tried to be more adult. More on top of the situation. He inhaled deeply attempting to choke back his crying. As he did, his young body shook and the tears flowed more freely. Finally he broke down completely and buried his head in his mother's lap as he sobbed and shook uncontrollably. She cradled him there gently stroking his hair, his body jerking rhythmically as he wept.

"You're a good boy, Tony," she whispered above the hiss of the nebulizer. "You're a good boy."

Chapter 5
Match of the Day

Tosh sat in the bath and soaked himself in a soapy paradise for an hour. Every time the water temperature dropped he turned on the hot tap with his big toe until his skin tingled. He turned the volume up full belt on his radio. It was heavy metal night on 96 FM. Megadeth pounded the airwaves with what sounded like a cacophony of clattering dustbin lids. They were followed by a new metallic sound from Clare called Vomit and Puke, and then the Dublin group with the name Bring Back Hanging for Fans of Elvis Presley. Tosh didn't think much of the music but he enjoyed listening to the names of the bands.

His legs bore the scars of the day's battle with Bishopstown. It had been a tough contest which they had lost by a point. Tosh was satisfied with his own performance. He scored two goals and five points. His last point came from a forty five. He had never pointed one of those before. He savoured the moment again as he stepped back to take that kick. The short run up then that beautiful moment of leather connecting with leather. Swoosh! How good he felt as he watched that ball sail over the bar to the applause of his team-mates and the scattering of spectators on the sidelines.

"Good man, Tosh!"

"Fair play to ya, Tosh!"

"Nice one, Tosh!"

"Wouldn't doubt ya, Tosh boy!"

"Come on the Heights!"

It was nice to dwell on the moment now in the heat of a relaxing bath. He hadn't been able to say much to Naylor about the match. Naylor had refused to discuss it. Gary had taken him off after ten minutes.

"Sod him anyway! He can go to blazes! That's the last time I ever turn up to play for him again! What does he know about football anyway? He's from friggin' Wexford!"

Tosh didn't comment except to tell him that they played football in Wexford too and that Gary had once been one of their finest players.

Gary had been right to take him off. He was playing a stinker! Firstly he gave away a penalty when he brought down an opposing forward who hadn't a hope of scoring. Then when Gary moved him up to the forward line he missed three clear chances in front of goal. Gary was left with no choice. There were at least four better players on the substitutes' bench ready to take his place.

Afterwards Tosh hadn't the heart to tell Naylor the truth. He would talk him around in a day or two. His pride was hurt. He'd get over it. By Tuesday he'd be ready to be told that he was unlucky to miss those chances and then he'd be raring to go to training.

Overall it had been a very pleasant day. A fabulous match, a great feed in the chipper and a good laugh with Naylor after mass. They had sat down on the church steps for ages talking about everybody they knew. They did that a lot. Naylor was a great mimic and he imitated all the teachers at Freemount Secondary to a tee with perfect accents and actions. They ambled home from church laughing and joking all the way.

"Tosh, I reckon she fancies you all right!"

"Who... Aisling?" Tosh wondered whether Naylor could mind-read as well as mimic!

"Not at all! Your one!"

"Who?"

"The old one you shook hands with at mass!"

"Get away!"

"She didn't say 'Peace be with you', she said, 'I'll have a piece of you'!"

Tosh was still laughing when he left Naylor on the stairway of the fourth floor.

"Give us a shout in the morning! We might go up and watch the soccer in Kilbarry."

"Sure thing! That's if you have nothing better to do! Toyboy!"

Tosh turned on the tap again and another gush of hot water made him sink deeper into thought. Aisling! What a gorgeous name. He hoped he was right and that she had been looking for him. He really liked her.

When he sat down next to her for science he always caught the scent of flowers. Roses. Once or twice he was tempted to sit a little closer so he could inhale her fragrance more deeply. He never did though. He was happy just to be near her for a whole double period. He often watched her as she took down experiment data from the blackboard. She had a habit of licking her upper lip as her eye moved from board to page. Class that!

And then there would be that wonderful time before each class would begin. Five minutes of conversation. She was so bright and cheerful. Witty too. She had a wonderful laugh. It was like a neverending giggle. The kind of laugh that made you want to join in too. She always parted her lips when she smiled revealing beautiful straight white teeth. It made Tosh want to stare at her.

She often asked him about himself and home. Tosh always felt comfortable telling her things. She wasn't being nosey. She was interested. She was the type of girl to whom you could tell things and be sure that she wouldn't discuss you with her friends later on. It was the day that Tosh told her about how his mother died that he really discovered how much he liked her. It was as if he had never told anybody before.

He recalled his father collecting him early from school. That had been strange. Dad never did the collecting. He said nothing all the way home. Tosh remembered telling him all the usual classroom gossip and how his father just smiled. He told him when they got home. The flat was full of relatives and friends all wearing troubled stares as they saw both father and son.

"Where's Mam?" Tosh remembered asking. It was then that his father took him out on to the balcony and told him to look up at the cloudless sky.

"Can you see that, son? Can you see the sky?"

"Yes, Dad. And the sun too!"

"That's where Mam lives now. She was too sick to live down here so Holy God took her up to his house."

"In heaven?"

"Yes, Tom, pet. Mam is in heaven."

"Can I see her, Dad?"

"No, love. But she can see you. So be a good boy and don't upset your mam by crying, sure you won't?"

Tosh remembered his father crying at that point so he joined in too. They cried a lot over the next few days. People he had never met before kept shaking his hand and telling him to be brave. That was weird. Any time he saw his father getting upset he got upset too until it got to the stage where neither could look at the other without tears being shed.

Then suddenly it was all over. It was just the two of them alone in the flat. There was no more crying. Mam was rarely mentioned again except for the odd reference. "Your mam would have loved *Coronation Street.*" "Your mother would have been so proud of you in your new school uniform!" "Would have" always seemed so sad.

Apart from Aisling he had never told this story to anybody else before. Not fully. Not like this. As he told her of how he lost his mother as a five-year-old he suddenly became anxious to fill in all the details. How he felt. Whom he saw. How his father reacted. The removal. The neighbours. The coffin. The wreaths. The burial. The single red rose. The mass cards. The tears. The sadness.

The memories came flooding back. The more he spoke the more he wanted to tell her and the more she wanted to listen. She listened tenderly. She looked at him all the time. Listening with her eyes. At times he had to divert his own eyes from hers. She didn't comment or say anything stupid or sentimental. She just told him that he had a great memory.

"Maybe you should write it all down some time. You could

write some poems about it all. Your dad would like that."

Write it down. Poems. Of course his dad would like it. What a class idea! What a classy lady!

He dried himself and covered himself with deoderant and talcum powder. He borrowed his dad's razor and scratched away the few faint hairs on his upper lip. He didn't really need to shave but it was nice to know that he was getting there. He splashed on some aftershave for good measure and inhaled deeply. He smelt good. Pity he was on his own!

He put on his clean jeans and his favourite baggy sweatshirt and turned off the radio. That was enough Vomit and Puke for one night. He took his essay notebook from his schoolbag and lifted the bundle of clothes from the kitchen table and placed them on the fridge. He would sort them later. It was a Saturday ritual. His father would do the ironing before going out and Tosh would sort them. With the table clear he sat down and took up his pen. He looked at the blank page in front of him and began to write. He had memorised the title since Friday. He wrote it at the head of the page.

"Pollution. What Pollution?"

He thought of his knacky subheading, then changed it again.

"Teatime on the Northside"

Kearney, his English teacher, would like that. He was a very funny man. He once brought them into the video room and showed them *The Commitments.* That was some laugh. The language was incredible. Afterwards they discussed the film from every angle. Tosh never realised that there was so much involved in film-making. Kearney was good at that. Making you think. Making you look further into things. Tosh liked that. He liked Kearney.

"As I polluted my body with 'high in cholesterol, low in nutrition', battered sausages, I couldn't decide which annoyed me most. Was it the noise from the vibrating bus engine or the filthy black fumes which it vomited into the air from its rusty exhaust... "

He stopped writing and re-read. He smiled. The image of exhaust fumes being vomited appealed to his sense of humour. He had been inspired by the heavy metal brigade from Clare. Continuing to write, he kept an eye on the clock. BBC1 were showing FA Cup highlights at twenty-past-ten. Liverpool had been beaten three-one at Chesterfield. This was a piece of sporting history. He wasn't going to miss it.

The words came easily. English was his favourite subject, especially writing. He wrote poems and stories which he kept in a box under his bed. He hadn't told anybody about them. He was afraid people might laugh. He had thought of telling Aisling because she had heard some that he had written for homework. She said they were really clever. But what if she didn't like these secret poems. That would be too embarrassing. She would be too polite to say so and then they would both end up feeling awkward. No. For the time being the poems would stay under the bed.

At ten-past-ten he wrote his last sentences.

"So with a stomach full of E-additives and indigestion, I decided to go to mass and pray for the salvation of the universe. I popped the empty coke can into the the bin at the back of the church. On Monday the children from St Peter's Primary would take it for recycling. I was doing my little bit! I looked up at a statue of Our Lord and I thought, 'I wonder can he see me now... through the gaping hole in the ozone layer!'"

He read the essay again. He was pleased. Especially the last bit. Kearney would laugh at that. Kearney was forever praising and encouraging him. Once he wrote at the bottom of an essay, "You not only have a gift for expressing thoughts, but for having thoughts worth expressing."

That made Tosh smile. If only he knew the half of it! Why wouldn't he have a head full of thoughts? He spent so much time on his own he had nothing else to do other than think!

He made a pot of tea and checked the biscuit tin. Great! Dad had filled it with fig rolls and chocolate chip cookies. He went into the sitting-room and turned on the telly. Perfect reception! The sporting hero of the Heights' Under Fourteens stretched out on the couch. It had been a long time since he had felt so satisfied. Dad would be home soon and they would probably stay up talking football into the small hours. He sighed with contentment. At a time like this he thought all was well with the world. He munched a biscuit as the *Match Of The Day* signature tune played. Ah yes! All is well! Roll on Chesterfield!

Chapter 6

Neighbours

The banging at the door startled him.

"Who in the name of God is there?" He roared as he made his way from his bedroom to the front door tying up his trousers en route.

"It's four o'clock in the morning!"

"It's the Gardai, Mr Twomey. Will you open the door please?"

"Guards? I've done nothing! What do you want with me?" came the confused reply.

"We know that, sir. We've got a bit of a problem and we think you might be in a position to help us out."

Ger Twomey slid back the bolt and unlocked the door. Standing there before him between two gardai was Naylor.

"Sorry for knocking you up in the middle of the night Mr Twomey but Tony here told us that you wouldn't mind. I'm Linda Creedon and this is Jack Dunphy. May we come in and explain?"

Ger Twomey was still confused but he ushered in his surprise guests and led them into the kitchen. He put the kettle on as they sat around the table and he waited for someone to tell him what the hell was going on.

"You're not in any sort of trouble are you, Naylor?" he asked.

"No, Mr Twomey... Mm... It's me Mam."

Linda took up the story.

"Mrs O'Neill was the victim of a very nasty assault earlier this evening. Her condition is stable."

"Assault? Who would want to assault Betty O'Neill?"

"That's what we hope to discover, Mr Twomey."

"Lousy thugs!" Ger Twomey was angry. "Dirty rotten thugs! Any one who would beat up a lady like Betty O'Neill deserves to be locked up with the key thrown in the Lee. By God if I could lay my hands on them I'd... Sorry, miss!"

"That's okay Mr Twomey. It's more than understandable that you might be angry. However that kind of talk won't help the situation."

"You're right, of course. My apologies. It's just that these people don't appear to have any standards. They can stoop so low. It makes me sick!"

"What's going on? Naylor? What are you doing here this hour of the night?"

Tosh had heard all the commotion and had come into the kitchen.

"Someone broke into the flat and beat up me mam," came the curt reply. Tosh shook his head in bewilderment.

"She's in the Regional. She's having an operation in the morning."

There followed a long pause as Naylor tried to hold back the tears and Tosh tried to take in the severity of the situation.

"You must be Tosh. Tony tells me you and he are great mates," said Linda breaking the silence. She then introduced herself and Jack. Ger made the tea and the tin of biscuits was placed in the middle of the table. Nobody said much. Ger made small talk with Linda and Jack while Tosh and Naylor sat in silence. Tosh knew he would get the full story later.

"That was a lovely cuppa, Mr Twomey. I'm afraid we have to go now. Would you mind looking after Tony for a day or two?"

"Tony can stay for as long as he likes."

"That's very good of you."

"Not at all. If the roles were reversed Betty O'Neill would be the first to help me out. She's the salt of the earth. As far as I'm concerned Tony stays for as long as it takes."

They moved to the front door. As Ger opened it Linda whispered to him.

"Mrs O'Neill is really very ill. We didn't tell Tony but they're actually operating on her at the moment. They're hoping to remove a clot from her brain."

"Oh holy God!"

"Just try and make sure Tony gets a good night's sleep and you can bring him to the hospital yourself tomorrow morning. If there's any change we'll obviously call before then. Goodnight Mr Twomey and thank you very much."

"Yeah, goodnight guards."

He locked the door and leaned with his back to it. From the kitchen he could hear the two lads chatting quietly. He sighed deeply and closed his eyes.

"Christ," he whispered. "Suffering Christ!"

Chapter 7
Dad

He was sitting in the kitchen eating a sandwich when Aisling arrived home from her cycle. He glanced at her and muttered a barely audible hello.

"Where were you, Dad?" she asked, thinking the question to be reasonable, considering he had been on the missing list for the past two days.

"Out!" he answered abruptly.

She noticed the letter was on the breakfast bar next to his plate. He had obviously read it but seemed unaffected by its contents.

"What are you going to do about Mum?" she asked.

He looked at her as he chewed for a moment then shrugged his shoulders.

"Is that a 'don't know' shrug or a 'don't care' shrug?"

"It's just a shrug. A twitch of the shoulders. The kind of thing you do when you don't want to continue with a conversation." He was being dismissive. Aisling hated that.

"What do you mean 'conversation'. We are not having a conversation. Two people have to talk in order to have a conversation and from where I'm standing that isn't happening!"

"Give me a break, Ais!"

"No I won't give you a break! I have been worried sick all day about this mess and all you can do is eat sandwiches and shrug your shoulders. Mum has gone, Dad! She has gone back to France! It's your fault! You caused this mess in the first place and if you want to get this family back together again then it's up to you to do something about it!"

Aisling stormed out of the room leaving her father to digest both the remains of his sandwich and her angry words. She locked her bedroom door behind her and threw herself onto her bed. She felt a sense of relief having spoken to him like that. For the past few months she had wanted to roar at him.

Her mother had done so. Screamed blue murder at times. Not that the screaming had had any effect.

Her father had changed since he had lost his job last year. He seemed to blame himself when Tronicworld, the multinational computer firm for which he had been the financial controller, pulled out of Ireland. In truth, he had nothing to do with the closure. The decision was made at the mother plant in Boston. He wasn't even consulted. However he kept saying that he should have been prepared. As chief accountant he should have picked up the warning signs. No amount of telling him that it wasn't his fault would placate him.

"Who the hell would want to employ me now? I'm the financial controller who lost control," he said one morning when Aisling and her mother begged him to apply for a position advertised in *The Irish Times*.

His personality soon went into decline. He became moody and irritable. He picked on Finbarr and Aengus for no apparent reason other than to give voice to his anger and frustration. Although never physically violent he would roar at them without provocation. Finbarr would never appear to react but his silence masked a deep sense of hurt. Aengus on the other hand would burst into tears and scream at his father begging him to stop.

Aisling's mother, too, fell victim to his moods. Aisling would lie awake at night and listen to their rows. It would begin with murmurs which would gradually rise to shouts and end with screaming and tears. How she wished it could all change and they could return to the days when the house was free of raised voices and heightened tensions.

He developed more silent tactics after a while. He would go weeks on end without speaking. Then he started his disappearing act. He would drive off in the morning and not return for two to three days. He never explained where he had been. He would just lapse into silence once again and a morose air would descend upon the house.

As Aisling lay on the bed her thoughts returned to the

letter which she had placed on the bedside locker. The more often she read it the more it all began to make sense. Her mother simply couldn't take any more. She had no choice. The boys were clearly affected by the upset in the house. The very least she could do was take them away from it all. Maybe moving to back to France would jolt her father back to common sense.

Aisling understood fully both why her mother hadn't told her in advance that she was leaving and why she didn't ask her to go with her and the boys. She knew that Aisling would have tried to talk her out of it and that there was no way she would have agreed to go. Instead she insisted in her letter that Aisling would move to her Aunt Una's house in Togher. Aisling smiled to herself. Sorry, Mum, but no way am I going to that house! Aunt Una was the type of aunt who treated all her nephews and nieces as if they had a mental age of sub four. She was better of with a depressed father than with somebody who was likely to feed her on diet of rusks and Care Bear videos.

From where she lay she could hear her father mount the stairs. She heard his bedroom door slam. At least for tonight she thought there will be no shouting.

Chapter 8

Monday Morning at Nine

The buzz of the assembly hall was typical of a Monday morning. Miss Connolly hadn't arrived yet and so groups of noisy teenagers huddled around the large timber floored hall.

Busy conversations were interlaced with adolescent laughter and the odd shriek of surprise or wonder. Even though it was a mixed school the groups were predominantly single-sexed. The boys tended to share the weekend news together while the girls too seemed to prefer their own company as they compared the state of play since Friday.

Aisling was pretending to listen to Pauline as she once again filled them in on the continuing saga of her love-life. As she rambled on about Brian, Eamonn and the quarterpounders, Aisling scanned the hall for Tosh. There he was! Sitting on the radiator with Naylor. She would have to talk to him. Would she walk up to him right now? That might look a bit odd. Maybe she should wait until they were in class. She might pretend to ask him for the loan of a biro and then quietly ask him to meet her at lunch break in the canteen. Or maybe she should slip him a written message. To hell! There was no time like the present!

"Aisling! Where are you off to?" cried Pauline in amazement.

"I'll be back in the minute," Aisling told her from halfway across the hall.

"Hi Tom! Hi Tony!"

Tosh and Naylor were surprised. They both mumbled something which sounded like hello.

"Did you have a good weekend?" she asked.

There was a silence. Aisling immediately felt as if she had asked the wrong question.

"Mmm... It was eventful, Aisling!" said Naylor, sensing the embarrassment.

"Oh? I hope it wasn't anything too bad."

"Well… I've had better weekends!" smiled Naylor.
"Naylor's mom was beaten up on Saturday. She's in hospital. Fractured skull, broken ribs, collar-bones and jaws, with internal bleeding for good measure." Tosh spelt out the details leaving no mystery.
"My God, that's awful, Tony! I'm so sorry!"
"Why?" smiled Naylor, "You didn't do it!" Naylor gave a nervous laugh. None of them found the remark in the slightest bit funny.
"That's really awful, though. Have the guards any idea who did it?"
"Not a clue!" said Tosh throwing his eyes up to heaven.
"They reckon it's drug-related. Kids breaking in to get money to buy drugs. If I could only get my hands who did it I'd leave them for dead!" Naylor told her.
"Bull!" said Tosh, "Pure and utter bull!"
"It's not, Tosh! I'm going to find out who did this and…"
"No, Naylor, I meant what the guards said about kids doing it was bull!"
"Why?" asked Aisling.
"Because… oh damn it, the bell. Listen, why don't you join Naylor and me for lunch and we'll tell you the whole story?"
"Great! Actually I was hoping to talk to you."
"To me?" Tosh felt suddenly elated.
"Yeah." Aisling looked at Naylor who felt suddenly excluded. "Oh and you, of course, Tony!" Naylor smiled but he knew Aisling was only being polite.
"I've got some problems of my own at the moment. So I'll see you guys later then!" she said as she turned to leave them.
"Sure! We could take a stroll to the park. It's a lot better than the canteen." Tosh beamed.
"Okay! We can slip away after maths. Bye!"
Aisling shuffled across the hall to rejoin her friends.
"I didn't know you fancied him!" said Pauline in an annoyed voice.
"Who?" asked Aisling innocently.

"Tom Twomey!"

"Who said anything about fancying him? I was only talking to himself and Naylor!" she smirked as she saw jealousy rise up in her friend. Good enough for her, she thought!

The scattered groups moved into more orderly class lines and sat on the plastic seats. Miss Connolly moved towards the microphone and wished them all a good morning. The buzzing of mixed conversations and laughter faded to silence as she read out the notices for the week. Aisling looked straight ahead unaware that Pauline was glaring at her. Tosh and Naylor sat directly behind them.

"You lousy sod!" whispered Naylor.

"What did I do?" asked Tosh.

"Inviting her to lunch! You knew full well that I'm going to the hospital to see me mam at lunch-time!"

"Oh that's right! Sorry, Naylor, I forgot!"

"Sorry me arse!"

"I'll tell her you were asking for her!"

Tosh reclined into his seat smirking to himself. He looked at Aisling's long dark hair hanging loosely down her back. From where he sat he was sure he could smell roses.

Chapter 9
Lunch

The park was practically deserted. In the play area a father was pushing his daughter on a swing while an elderly man sat reading his newspaper on one of two park benches. Tosh and Aisling shared the other. They ate tentatively. Each was somewhat in awe of the other. Naylor seemed the common ground on which to break the ice.

"His mother must have taken a terrible beating," said Aisling opening the conversation.

"She sure did! We were up there yesterday. You wouldn't recognise her. Her face is all twisted. It's all purple and bloated," replied Tosh. "She can't talk because both her jaws are wired up. She just lies there staring into space. Still, the consultant called in the afternoon and told us she was out of danger. She's coming out of intensive care this morning."

"That's a relief. Why did you say this morning that the guards were wrong when they said it was local kids who were doing it?"

"Sharks did it," stated Tosh in a matter-of-fact sort of way.

"Sharks?"

"Loan sharks. They're all over the place. They offer you money. You pay some of it back. They then offer you a top up to help pay off the first loan. It rolls on and on like that until they own you."

"Did Naylor's mother owe a lot?"

"I don't know exactly how much but I reckon she was in too deep. You see, Aisling, when you're living on social welfare your life is all about waiting for Thursday. When you get your money you pay off some of your debt, then the rest is yours. But you realise that what's left isn't enough so you borrow some more. Then you wait until Thursday when you have two more debts to clear. It's not long until you're in too deep."

"But surely it's all highly illegal. You can't just beat somebody up because they can't pay you what you owe!"

"That's the trouble. The loaning company might be above board. But then you have the private lenders. The sharks. They're the boys who cause the grief. Nobody ever sees them. They send out the heavies. They've never heard of interest rates. It's a case of we give you fifty, you give us a hundred."

"That's awful!"

"They wait around outside the dole office on a Thursday and on the first Tuesday of every month they follow women home from the post office after they've collected the childrens' allowance. The trouble is Naylor is out for revenge. He has his heart set on getting these guys back for what they did. I'm not sure how he is going to do it without getting himself killed in the process!"

Aisling was impressed with Tosh. She had known nothing of this way of life. It was a whole new world to her. In a peculiar way it also excited her.

"How do you know all this, Tosh?"

"When you live in the Heights, Aisling, you grow up pretty fast. You learn things that school will never teach you."

"Do you know any of these sharks?"

"No!" Tosh laughed. " They don't exactly leave calling cards or wear identity badges."

"Is there anything we could do?"

"How do you mean?"

"Like finding out who the heavies are who beat up Mrs O'Neill. Surely we could do something!"

Aisling was putting thoughts into Tosh's head. Frightening thoughts! Dangerous thoughts!

"Well, as I told you, Naylor's hell-bent on finding out who did it! There's no way he'll be able to do it all on his own. Maybe we could sniff around alright. It might be a bit dodgy though. I'll have a chat with him afterwards at the hospital... Here try one of these!"

Tosh handed Aisling a jaffa cake. The conversation was heading in the right direction. He was happy. She was saying that they might do something together. That was music to his ears. She said "we"! Tosh and Aisling! Together! The fact that she was suggesting that they investigate the activities of possibly a gangster organisation wasn't exactly romantic but it was a start. She liked jaffa cakes too. Thank God he threw them into his bag that morning! Tosh was beginning to enjoy this picnic. They ate in silence for a while until Tosh suddenly remembered that Aisling had mentioned a problem of her own before assembly.

"What was it you wanted to talk to me about this morning?" he asked. She didn't answer. She kept chewing her biscuit. It wasn't that she was avoiding the question. Far from it, she had been anxious to tell him about it all weekend. However, now at the critical point of breaking the silence, she wasn't quite sure how to word it all.

"You said you had some sort of a problem yourself," Tosh enquired, mistaking Aisling's silence for forgetfulness or perhaps simply not hearing him.

"Tosh," she began but paused.

"Yes?"

"It's my parents. They've split up. My mother walked out on Saturday. She took Finbarr and Aengus with her and has gone to her own mother in Bordeaux." She felt relieved. It was out! At last she was telling somebody.

"I'm sorry, Aisling." Tosh wasn't sure what to say. "I never thought you had any problems at home. I mean... you never let on... "

"Well there was never any major hassle up until the last year or so. After dad lost his job. Then it all happened so suddenly. Dad became a different person. The arguments were happening every night. I suppose all along I was expecting him to get a job and that everything would get back to normal again."

"Why didn't your mother bring you to France?" asked Tosh, who was grateful that Mrs O'Gorman hadn't!

"She knew I wouldn't agree to go. Well not without finishing the school year first. She did say in the letter that she wants me over for Easter and that I might join her for good after the summer."

"Oh," said Tosh, who was missing her already! "I suppose you mightn't have much of a choice then."

"I hope things will have sorted themselves out at that stage. It's up to Dad really. I'm sure if he gets his act together Mum will come back and try again."

"You're sure?"

"Well no. I just hope so, that's all!"

"What's she going to do in France?" Tosh asked.

"She's gone to stay with my grandmother. Gran has been ill lately. She had a stroke last year. She's made a good recovery. She got her speech back and she can walk again but she finds the restaurant a bit too much to handle on her own. Mum has gone to help her."

"How did your Dad react?"

"To Mum leaving?"

"Yeah."

"I don't think he reacted at all. He found out the same way I did. Mum left him a note."

Aisling explained about how she found her father sitting eating his sandwich after having read his wife's letter. She told Tosh how unconcerned he seemed and how she blew a fuse and told him what she thought of him. She felt good telling him these things. The burden she had been carrying for the weekend seemed to lift from her shoulders and for some strange reason the pain of her parents' separation had eased somewhat.

"It's been great talking to you about these things, Tosh."

"Don't mention it. All I did was listen!"

"Yeah I know but it was great having somebody who actually listens. I was really lonely since Saturday, but I feel a lot better now." She smiled a delicious smile at him and Tosh was sure that her teeth sparkled. He wanted to reach across and meet the smile with a kiss but he was afraid she might take it the wrong way. Better not risk it, he thought. She likes me and that's good enough. For now.

"Will you come to my place for an hour after school?" she asked. "I can cook us some tea and we could play some CDs."

“That’d be great, and then we might both go over to the Regional to see Naylor. My Dad and he will be there at about six.”

“Okay,” she smiled.

“Great!” he said.

They finished their lunch without talking. The little girl on the swing was telling her daddy she was tired and wanted to go home. The old man on the next bench also decided to leave, obviously feeling the pinch of the chilly February breeze. Tosh stood up and walked to the river bank. He fed the crusts and crumbs to the grateful ducks. Aisling joined him.

“They don’t get too many extra snacks this time of year,” he told her as the ducks cackled and quacked in a huddled group, each jostling and scavenging for a share of the spoils.

“We’ll have to come and feed them more often,” she added.

“Sure!” smiled Tosh. He liked the sound of that!

Chapter 10
Bussing It

Naylor was annoyed with Tosh but he didn't want to show it. They sat upstairs on the number eight bus as it shuffled noisily along the Western Road on its way to the city centre. Tosh's dad sat behind them with his head buried in a novel he had picked up in the shop at the hospital. Both he and Naylor had spent the evening there. Tosh was supposed to have joined them but apparently had become sidetracked by Aisling.

"I'm sorry, Naylor! She asked me to call around after school for an hour but one thing led to another… "

"Oh yeah!" said Naylor trying to sound totally uninterested.

"Yeah!" said Tosh. "She was down in the dumps. Her parents have just split up and she wanted somebody to talk to!"

Ger Twomey laughed suddenly from behind them! He leaned forward and began to mimic.

"Tired, lonely, depressed, suicidal? Don't contact the Samaritans, give my son a call, the amazing Tom Twomey, the teenage agony aunt!"

Naylor laughed along with him.

"Haw haw! Very funny, Dad! Just read your book!"

"I would if I didn't have to listen to your ramblings."

"They aren't ramblings. Aisling is a good friend of mine and she needed a bit of company. Hey, Naylor!" Tosh's voice grew excited. "You should have seen the house… "

"I'm not interested!" Naylor was wearing one of those "call yourself a friend?" pouts. He was battling hard to show no enthusiasm. He was failing miserably. He was dying to find out all about Tosh's day with Aisling. A long pause followed as Tosh looked haughtily out of the window and Naylor's curiosity was getting the better of his attempted indifference.

"So… did you meet Mr O'Gorman?" asked Naylor, his curiosity finally breaking.

"Yeah, he was there. He didn't say much, though. He just asked me about football and stuff. Told me he was more of a rugby man himself. Aisling reckons he's going through a tough time himself at the moment. Depression. He lost his job last year and he's had some sort of personality change ever since."

Ger Twomey looked up from his book and leaned forward again.

"That happens. I saw a programme on Channel Four last week all about that. 'Yuppie Blues' it was called. It was all about these business men who find themselves out of work. Apparently they find it much harder to cope than ordinary unemployed people."

"I saw that too!" added Naylor. "It was brilliant... "

Naylor and Ger suddenly launched into a full scale discussion on the programme they had both seen. Tosh made a mental note to watch more documentaries as he listened to his friend and his father having a political debate on the different effects of unemployment. Still, he was happy to let them ramble on. It allowed his own mind to wander. As the bus nosed its way though the busy southside streets, Tosh sat back and reflected on his day.

The house was magic. Rooms everywhere! He loved the conservatory best of all. It was full of potted plants with these great big floral-cushioned wicker seats and a glass-topped coffee table in the shape of the map of Ireland. They sat there and ate their burgers which Aisling had made. Even though it was freezing outside the glass walls seemed to soak in the February sunshine making it warm and cosy. The burgers were lovely. She made them with real mincemeat and put lashings of coleslaw and lettuce on them. Tosh ate two with a huge plate of chips.

They talked all the time and Aisling seemed to be really pleased that that he had gone there with her. He quite liked Mr O'Gorman. He wasn't at all as Tosh had imagined. He looked really young. He didn't notice any depression either. He was a bit on the quiet side but he was very welcoming and polite.

"He doesn't seem that bad to me, Aisling," said Tosh when Mr O'Gorman had gone out for a walk.

"Of course not. He would never let on to a stranger that there would be anything wrong. I heard him telling his sister, my Aunt Una, on the phone that Mum had gone to France to visit Gran as she had taken a bit of a turn. He wants everything to appear as normal," Aisling explained as she loaded the plates into the dishwasher.

"Una, that's the aunt in Togher your mother wants you to move in with for a while."

"Yeah, that's her. But there's no bloody way I'm going there!"

"Why not?"

"Una is my godmother, Tosh. She still treats me as if I'm an infant. I stayed there last year and she asked me would I like a bedtime story! She gave me Ready Brek for breakfast! Can you imagine?"

Tosh laughed out loud. Aisling liked the sound of his laughter. She was glad it was she who had caused it.

"Anyway it's not just the fact that Una treats me like I should be in a play-pen that stops me going there," she added when Tosh had stopped laughing.

"No?"

"No, it's Dad. He wants me to go there, too. That would really suit him at the moment. He'd be able to disappear again. He wouldn't dare do that if I was here on my own. So I'm staying put."

"Yeah," agreed Tosh. "That makes sense."

Tosh hadn't noticed the time slipping by. It was quarter-past-six and he had promised Naylor he would be at the hospital for six.

"I've got to go, Aisling. I'm dead late. Naylor will murder me! I'll get a half-six bus into town and then a seven o'clock out to the hospital.

"I won't join you, Tosh, if you don't mind. Dad seems a bit brighter today. Maybe talking to you about sport brought him out of himself. He was quite a sportsman in his day."

"Yeah, he told me. Played for Munster against the All Blacks!"

"He was being modest. He has three Irish caps as well."

"Wow!" Tosh was impressed.

"Anyway, I'll try and get him to talk to me when he comes back. Maybe I'll get him to open up."

"Good idea, Aisling," agreed Tosh. "I'll be off so!"

"Why don't you take Finbarr's bike?"

It was then that Tosh got embarrassed. He politely refused, having thanked her for the offer. Aisling dismissed his refusal assuring him that it would be a great idea. Tosh tried to make excuses but she wasn't taking no for an answer.

"I insist!" she told him as he kept saying that he couldn't possibly.

"Maybe your old fella might get narked. You know the way he is at the moment. The least little thing might... "

"Dad won't mind at all. There are two bikes there so Naylor can borrow the other one. It'll be much easier for the pair of you to get to and from the hospital!"

He decided to come out with it as he felt his embarrassment was beginning to show.

"Err... The thing is, Aisling... I can't cycle!" He waited for her to react but she just smiled.

"I hope I didn't embarrass you, Tosh!"

"No not at all!" he lied "It's funny isn't it, there are kids living around the Heights and they've been robbing BMWs since they were ten and I'm fourteen and I can't ride a two-wheeler!"

Aisling laughed. Tosh blushed but he was glad he told her.

"Come on Tosh!" she told him as she took him by the hand and led him out of the house to the shed where the bikes were kept. He liked the feel of her hand in his. Her skin was really soft. Like silk. Even her nails felt soft. Despite the frosty weather he felt warm inside. She made him sit up on the saddle while she held the back wheel steady.

"Now keep your balance and pedal slowly. Once you get

into your stride, pedal a little faster and I'll let go," she instructed.

Tosh got it in one and was cruising up and down the garden path in no time. He loved the sound the wheels made when he braked on the gravel. Even though he was tempted he decided against taking the bike to the hospital.

"No, I'll get the bus," he told her reluctantly. "Besides, me dad and Naylor will be there and I'll bus it home with them. But I'll come around tomorrow if you like and I'll take it then."

"Great! I'll give you a second lesson then!" she promised with that warm wide smile.

Tosh was beaming from ear to ear. Sometime in the not-to-distant future, he thought to himself, I'm going to tell her that I can't swim!

"Up you get, Tosh, this is our stop!" announced Naylor as number eight pulled into Patrick Street. They had to change to get the number three home to the Heights. The bus wasn't there as usual. They waited at the stop each of them shuffling to keep warm as the the night air plummeted below freezing.

"That bloody bus won't be here for another hour, I think we'll walk the bus route. We'll probably be home before it!" suggested Ger.

"Yeah I think you're right, Dad. We'll turn into snowmen if we stay here any longer."

They walked briskly to the top of Patrick Street and turned left towards the Christy Ring Bridge. It was about ten to eight and the quays were busy with pedestrians heading to the Opera House for some play or other.

" The Man From Clare by John B. Keane'," read Tosh from the neon light noticeboard above the main doors of the theatre. "What's that about, Dad?"

"I think it's about a football team," said Ger. "Hang on, I bought a paper this evening in the Regional but I never got a chance to open it. I'll just see what it says about this famous 'Man From Clare'."

Ger took his newspaper under a bright orange street light and scanned the pages. Some article must have suddenly caught his attention as he stopped and began to read. It was clear from the shocked expression on his face that he was not reading from the entertainment's page.

"What is it, Mr Twomey?" asked Naylor. "You look as if you've seen a ghost!"

"You're nearly right, Naylor boy!" came the reply from a stunned Ger Twomey. The paper hung loosely from both of his hands.

"Dad! What's up?"

"Axle O'Callaghan is dead!"

"Christ!" gasped Naylor. "I didn't hit him that hard, did I?"

Chapter 11

Home Again

She was glad that Tosh had stayed so long. It was nice having him to talk to. He made her laugh. He was very amusing about not being able to cycle even though he was obviously a little bit embarrassed.

"Maybe you have an old one in the shed with stabilisers!" he said. "Or a trike!"

He promised to take Finbarr's bike after school the following day and Naylor could take Aengus's. They were both the same. Mountain bikes which her Mum and Dad had bought them for Christmas. It was just a question of raising the saddles and in Naylor's case this would hardly be necessary. Tosh told her that the bikes would be quite safe in the Heights as each flat had a basement shed fitted with a metal door.

After Tosh had left she made out a shopping list and headed to the shopping mall. Her father had asked her to do so before he left.

"Just get the usual stuff and an evening newspaper. See can you pick up an *Irish Times* too. I've left some money on the hall stand," he told her politely as she and Tosh tucked into their tea and he headed out for a stroll.

She was glad he had asked her to buy newspapers. Maybe he would look up the Situations Vacant columns.

She didn't spend much time shopping. Tosh had stayed longer than she had expected and she wanted to be home before her father. He had been in slightly better humour today. This might be a good time to talk to him about getting Mum home. Even though she had seen the headline, YOUTH DEAD, as she bought the newspapers she hadn't taken much notice.

She had just tidied the kitchen and put away the groceries when he arrived home. He came into the kitchen and stood at the doorway.

"Hi, Dad!" she said, offering a friendly opening.

"Hi, Ais!"

"Listen, Dad, I'm sorry about what I said on Saturday night, it was just... "

"No, Ais, it's me who should apologise... "

"No, Dad! I was wrong! I shouldn't have said what I... "

"Aisling!" he interrupted her before she began to grovel.

"Go into the sitting-room. We must have a chat. I'll be in shortly."

Aisling did as she was told. She sat and waited for her father who emerged some minutes later with a tray of tea and biscuits.

"Now!" he said. "As my mother used to say in times of crisis, 'Let's have a nice cup of tea!'"

They both laughed and Aisling felt relieved. It was a long time since her father had behaved so warmly towards her. He poured out two cups of tea and added milk into both knowing that she liked only the merest drop in hers. There was a long silence as they sipped their tea, each waiting for the other to say something.

"I suppose you think I've been a bit of a pain lately, Ais, don't you?" He wasn't seeking an answer and as she couldn't have said anything other than "As a matter of fact, yes," she just looked at him hoping for him to continue.

"The fact is I knew all along that I was making everybody feel miserable but there was nothing I could do about it. I knew I was upsetting everybody but it got to a stage where I couldn't control myself. Your mother tried to help me to snap out of it but I just couldn't. I was so used to being in charge. In control. Then suddenly it all disappears. I find myself out of work. No prospects. From top office to dole office in one swoop! I simply couldn't stop myself from feeling depressed. I suppose I wanted you all to share my hurt, to join in and be miserable with me."

"But you could have looked for another job, Dad," Aisling offered, without sounding critical.

"I did, love."

"When?"

"All those times I went missing. I was chasing after contacts. Former colleagues of mine. Guys I worked with or was in college with. Fellows I played rugby with. I travelled the length and breadth of the country knocking on doors trying to talk my way into a new position. But it was all a great waste of time. Nobody wanted to know."

"But you never said so, Dad. Any time Mum or me asked you where you had been you never said. Why?"

"I don't know. Shame perhaps. Or maybe I found it too difficult to admit defeat. To admit that I had failed. I didn't have the guts to face up to the fact that I could do something wrong. I remember the day I found out. The managing director put his head around my office door and handed me a memo. 'From Boston!'" he announced as he waved it to me. From the grin on his face you'd swear he was handing me a Christmas card. Apparently all the employees got the same one. It told us all in black and white that Tronicworld was ceasing its interests in Ireland as and from the close of business on Friday. That was it. As cold as that."

"That was awful, Dad!" Aisling told him. "Not even an apology?"

"No. Not even a courteous thank you. Later that day I was going to my car when a group of guys who worked on the assembly line spotted me. They started shouting angrily at me. As if it was all my fault. As if it was my decision, as financial controller, to close the plant down. They would never have believed me that I knew no more than themselves. The funny thing is I had just finished a report recommending that the company should consider expanding. Business was booming. I reckoned we could have taken on a hundred or so new workers no problem."

"So why did they pull out?" asked Aisling.

"That, Ais, is a very good question. I think they decided to move the Irish end of their operation to Mexico where basically they could get away with paying less taxes and lower wages to workers."

"Can they do that?"

"They just did, love! Anyway getting back to your mother and me. I just want to tell you that I realise now how stupid I've been. I gave her a terrible time, Ais. I took out all my anger and frustration on her. She couldn't take any more, and who could blame her? I gave Finbarr and Aengus a hard time too. I feel so guilty now for hurting them... " He paused and looked at his daughter.

"And for hurting you, Ais. I'm sorry."

Aisling shook her head and told him it was okay.

"I wish they'd come home, Ais. I miss them."

"Don't tell me, Dad! Phone mum and tell her."

"I did so this morning."

"And?" Aisling watched him anxiously.

"Your mother has suffered a hell of a lot, Ais. Don't expect her to come rushing home just because I'm... " he paused seeming unable to finish. Aisling helped him.

"Just because you're what, Dad?"

He sighed deeply. "Just because I'm sorry. I told her I was sorry. I told her that I realise now how stupid and selfish I have been." He paused for a while and then looked at Aisling. "I asked her to come home."

Aisling felt a rush of excitement. "And is she?"

"Not at the moment, love, no. She's not convinced. She didn't run away just to give me a fright. She needs time to think things over. She can't do that here, love. So let's give her that time, eh?"

Aisling was deflated. It was all too good to be true. Her father talking to her like that. His mood suddenly improved. He sounded positive for the first time since losing his job. It was hoping for too much that her mother would hop on the first plane home so they could all play happy families again. She got up, said goodnight and headed towards the stairs.

"Aisling!" he called as she left the room.

"Yes?"

"Thanks, love. You've been a great help. You made me open my eyes and stop feeling sorry for myself. Oh and by the way,

I think Tosh is a nice lad."

She smiled.

"Yeah, he's nice okay! Goodnight, Dad."

She went to bed that night feeling better. She lay in bed picturing her mother and the boys. Her mind wandered from the last conversations she had with her mother to the one she had just had with her father. She was exhausted but her mind refused to wind down. She tried to figure out whether she was feeling happy or sad. Was it optimism or pessimism? Before sleep overcame her jumbled kaleidoscope of thoughts she thought of Tosh on the bicycle. "He's nice okay," she whispered.

Chapter 12
The Removal

It took Naylor a long time to realise that he did not kill Axle O'Callaghan. His head-butt might have been his most violent act to date but it was far from lethal. Axle died having inhaled toxic substances. The post-mortem revealed he died as a result of respiratory failure due to solvent abuse. His friends who were with him when he died were more basic in their description of what happened. He choked on his own vomit after doing glue and petrol.

Naylor and Tosh left training early. Gary was peeved.

"The final is on in two weeks time. Any guy who misses training will be dropped. I don't care how good he thinks he is!" he snapped.

"For God's sake, Gary, we've got to go to the removal. Axle O'Callaghan is from the Heights. He was a neighbour of ours!" Tosh told him as he whipped off his football boots and threw them into his gear bag.

"Axle O'Callaghan was a wart on the face of humanity! He was a no-good vandal who spent his days making life miserable for himself and all those who came into contact with him. If you want my opinion we're all better off... "

"I don't want your opinion, Gary! You're not one of us! So go back to your yuppie apartment and shove your opinions up your filofax!" Naylor screamed at his manager taking him completely by surprise. Gary lived in the fashionable River Bank apartments in the city centre, a fact which always irritated Naylor.

"Naylor's right," Tosh came to his friend's support. "Whatever you think about Axle doesn't matter, Gary. He came from the Heights. We went to primary school with him and we're going to his funeral. If you want to drop me or Naylor for the final then go ahead. It's only a bloody game!"

Tosh calmly handed Gary his training singlet and walked out of the dressing-room. Naylor felt better for his outburst.

He had wanted to tell Gary what he thought of him for ages. Now that he had done so gave him a new sense of power. He handed him his singlet with a "don't you ever mess with me again" stare glaring from behind his thick-rimmed glasses.

"Do you think he will drop you, Tosh?" asked Naylor as they made their way to the funeral home in Shandon Street.

"No," replied Tosh. "But I reckon you'll be watching the game from the dugout! I couldn't believe you'd say that to him!"

"He made me mad, Tosh! Who the hell does he think he is? Just because he owns his own bakery and lives in that fancy apartment! That doesn't give him the right to look down on the rest of us!"

"He wasn't too fond of Axle, was he?" grinned Tosh.

"That's because Axle borrowed his car one night and took it to Killarney for a spin! It was his own fault. He left the keys in the ignition outside the Heights! What did he expect?"

"I don't think he'll be giving a graveside oration at the burial tomorrow!" They both laughed as they hurried along.

From the top of Shandon Street they saw a huge crowd congregating outside the funeral home. It seemed as if the whole of McGillicuddy Heights had come to pay tribute to Axle O'Callaghan. In truth most of the people there would have felt the same way as Gary about Axle. Tosh and Naylor both hated him when he was alive. In recent months this hatred gave way to fear. Axle was a dangerous character when he was high and both Tosh and Naylor avoided him like the plague. However, now that he was dead, fear and hatred were put to one side. All seemed united in expressing their sorrow to the O'Callaghan family in this their moment of loss.

Naylor's knees trembled when he saw the coffin. From the doorway he could see the pale face of the corpse jutting out in profile. As both he and Tosh approached his heart beat wildly. He partially closed his eyes hoping that he wouldn't have to look too closely when it was their turn to pass. However when their turn arrived Naylor's eyes seemed to pop themselves open and he stared at the dead face of Axle. He didn't look dead at all. He was wearing a blue suit and he seemed much cleaner than Naylor had ever remembered. Over his nose was a blue patch. Naylor felt guilty. Jesus, he thought. I did that! Thankfully the crowds behind them were pushing forward and they didn't get to view the deceased for too long. They moved outside into the fresh air as the priest picked up the microphone and called on everybody to pray for the soul of Alexander O'Callaghan.

"I never knew his name was Alexander! Did you, Tosh?"

"I doubt it if he knew himself!" whispered Tosh as they made their way from the funeral home to the shop across the road. From where they sat, eating their Mars bars and sipping their cokes, they could hear the prayers being chanted in murmured tones. Neither felt like joining in. The sight of Axle lying there in his coffin had left them both a little numb. Both preferred the relative safety of where they sat rather than the eerie proximity to the mortal remains of the infamous Alexander.

When the praying stopped there was much shuffling as people appeared to pour out onto the street. The early evening air buzzed with subdued conversations as neighbours gathered in groups and engaged in the usual funeral gossip.

"Sure, wasn't it an awful shock for his poor mother?"

"The poor child didn't know what he was at! He had no sense, God love him!"

"He was a grand lad behind it all you know!"

"There was great nature in him all the same."

"Salt of the earth!"

Tosh and Naylor wouldn't have agreed with all the praise the late Alexander was receiving but they certainly weren't going to voice any disagreement. Indeed as the coffin was shouldered out of the funeral parlour and placed carefully into the hearse they both found themselves joining in the blessings.

"God bless him and protect him," said a sobbing old lady standing beside the two lads.

"Amen," said Tosh.
"Amen," said Naylor.
"We won't see his likes again!" offered an old man as he sucked on a Woodbine and nodded his head as if he was agreeing with himself.
Thank God for that, thought Naylor and Tosh simultaneously.
Axle's two other brothers, Sledge and Mattie, were the last to emerge from the funeral parlour. They came out with their heads bowed solemnly. They each wore an ill-fitting grey suit with a white shirt and black tie. Both had large black circles under their red rimmed eyes. It was impossible to deduce whether this was a result of tears or of endless hours sniffing toxic substances. It was more likely that the one had emphasised the other.

Tosh and Naylor didn't get a chance to speak to the two brothers until after the burial the following morning. The two were surrounded by people shaking their hands and telling them that they were sorry for their troubles. When most of these sympathisers had left Tosh and Naylor decided it was their turn. Neither of them was looking forward to speaking to the O'Callaghan brothers. Remembering the events of the previous Saturday night Naylor was particularly wary.
"What's Sledge's real name?" whispered Tosh from the side of his mouth as they approached the two brothers.
"Hammer," muttered Naylor without smiling.
"Listen, Sledge," began Tosh. "I'm really sorry about Axle."
"Me too," added Naylor. "Sorry, Mattie. Oh and Sledge, I'm sorry about Saturday night.
"What about Saturday night?" grunted Sledge who even in a moment of mourning was still capable of grunting like the Terminator.
"You know! In the laneway when I gave you a knee between the..." he whispered the last bit out of respect for the occasion.
"You did what?" Sledge seemed totally at a loss.
"In the laneway. Me mam had been beaten up and I was

running to the payphone. You and your gang tried to stop me."

Suddenly there was a look of recall behind Sledge's misty eyes. He began to nod his head slowly grunting in time with each nod.

"I just want to say... no hard feelings... eh?"

Naylor gave Sledge a pleading look. He knew he was at his mercy. He was sorry he had brought the subject up in the first place as Sledge had been so spaced out he certainly had not remembered. Why didn't he just keep his mouth closed? Why couldn't he have just sympathised and moved away? Now that he had reminded Sledge of the incident he had given him an excuse to exact revenge at a later date. Not that an animal like Sledge would need an excuse. If it moved then it was a fair target in Sledge's way of thinking.

"I'm glad you reminded me of that, Naylor boy!" he boomed in yet another animalistic grunt.

"Don't mention it, Sledge!" said Naylor, even though what he really meant was "Please don't mention it, Sledge".

"No, because I knew I had something to tell you."

"You have something to tell me?" Naylor was surprised. It was a worried state of surprise!

"Yeah. It's about your mother."

They were interrupted by Father O'Leary who had come to make sure the two brothers were all right after the ordeal of the funeral.

"Well, boys. Is everything okay?"

"Fine, Father," said Mattie.

"We'll be fine, Father," said Sledge. "Thanks for everything."

"Come on and I'll give you a lift back to the Heights. I want to have a little chat with the two of you. There are one or two guys from the newspapers hanging around the place and I want to make sure that they don't get a chance to try and interview you. They've already written some horrible things about poor Alexander. Tony and Tom, are you all right for a lift?"

"Yes thanks, Father." said Tosh. They had taken Aisling up on the offer of the bikes and had cycled to the graveyard.

Before he left with Father O'Leary, Sledge whispered to Naylor who nodded enthusiastically.

"What did he say to you?" asked Tosh.

"He said he'd meet us in the afternoon above at the Tracks!"

"The Tracks! Good God! Naylor, I hope you realise what we could be letting ourselves in for!"

Chapter 13

The Tracks

"No way, Aisling! You don't know what you are talking about!" Tosh was being blunt.

"And what do you think is going to happen to me?" Aisling's voice was angry. "For God sake Tosh we're meeting him at four o'clock in the afternoon. It will be broad daylight. You and Naylor will be there too!"

"Look, Aisling, you just don't understand. The O'Callaghans are not normal human beings. There is no telling how they will react to us, let alone a pretty-looking girl like you!"

"Don't be such a sexist pig, Tosh!" she snapped, spitting the words into his face. Wow, that hurt!

"I'm not sexist!"

"You surely are! The only reason why you don't want me to go is that I'm a female. There is no other reason!"

"The only reason I'm going is for Naylor's sake. Believe me, if I could stay out of this one myself I would!"

"Fine! You stay here and Naylor and I will go on our own!"

Tosh was beginning to see another side to Aisling. They had been sitting in the kitchen of the flat drinking coffee. Aisling had a half day and had decided to come around for a chat. Tosh and Naylor had got permission to go to the funeral and hadn't been to school at all that morning.

"Sounds good to me!" said Naylor, who relished the chance of going off alone with Aisling – even if it was like venturing into a lion's den!"

"No bloody way!" Tosh eyed his friend with a "one more word out of you and you're dead" stare. Naylor picked up on the vibe without a second prompting.

"On second thoughts, Aisling, it might be better if Tosh and I went alone. He is right, you know. Those O'Callaghans are a bunch of savages!"

"I rather like to make my own mind on that after I've met

them, Naylor. Now how do we get to these 'Tracks'?"

"The Tracks" was a popular cider party venue. It was a disused railway station situated behind McGillicuddy Heights. It was reached by climbing a steep embankment and then scaling a wall, the top of which was enmeshed in barbed wire and speckled with imbedded fragments of glass. To gain access to the Tracks without cutting oneself in the process was a sport in itself.

At five-to-four Aisling, Naylor and Tosh were at the foot of the embankment. The misty weather had made the embankment slippery. Tosh went first but it took him three attempts to scamper to the top and grab on to a rock at the end of the wall. Naylor went next and was glad to catch Tosh's outstretched hand to help him up the last metre.

"Just take a run at it, Aisling, and reach for my hand!" Tosh was trying to be helpful but Aisling snarled.

"Listen, Chris bloody Bonnington, I think I can manage to get up that grass pimple without the assistance of Mountain Rescue, thank you very much!"

To the amazement of the pair at the top of the embankment, Aisling turned her back on them and calmly walked up backwards. Carefully she dug her heels in with each step and was standing alongside them in seconds. She then proceeded to scale the wall and jumped over the other side before Tosh or Naylor had figured out how they were going to avoid cutting their hands.

"Hurry up, you two!" she called teasingly as they groaned and rubbed their wounds before jumping down to join her.

"Now lads! Where do we go from here?" she asked.

Tosh's immediate response was to say "home" but he realised now that there was no way of getting out at this stage. He pointed to the disused hut on the far side of the tracks. Just as he did so a train hurtled out of the tunnel with its horn blaring at them to get back away from the tracks. Instantly the three fell backwards onto the grass bank where they rolled over in a human ball as the train thundered on its way.

"Christ, I must get new glasses! I never saw that train coming!" laughed Naylor as he picked himself up from the grass.

"Me heart!" said Tosh. "I thought we were all finished that time!"

They crossed the tracks quickly and entered the hut. The door was bolted closed with a rusty padlock hanging loosely from a chain. The side window was broken just enough for a body to squeeze through.

"Will I go first?" asked Naylor, hoping that Tosh would volunteer.

"No, it's okay. I will. Give me a leg up, Aisling."

Tosh stood into Aisling's cupped hands and hoisted himself onto the window ledge. Once there he reached down and pulled her up to join him.

"I'll go in, Aisling. You pull Naylor up and then follow me down."

Apart from the narrow beams of light which crept into the hut via the cracks in the timber door and the pocket of daylight from the high window, the hut was pitch black inside. Tosh held his breath as the stench of stale cider and urine was overpowering.

"Hold your nose when you come in here!" he shouted to the other two before they jumped from the ledge.

"Ugh! This place is like an open sewer!" complained Aisling as she tried to regulate her breathing.

Naylor took out the small torch he had been carrying in his pocket. He switched it on and shone it on the walls of the hut. The graffiti bounced off the light. Various vulgar messages were highlighted by the torch as it moved up and down each wall. Naylor fixed his spotlight on one with a chilling significance.

"AXLE WOS HEAR!"

"For God's sake, Naylor, turn that thing off!" barked Tosh as if the semi-literate message contained some kind of haunting presence. They sat together on an old desk and waited for Sledge and company to join them. After a few minutes their eyes became accustomed to the darkness and shady grey images came into focus.

"Stop doing that, Tosh!" whispered Aisling in an embarrassed tone.

"Doing what?" asked Tosh.

"Rubbing my thigh like that!"

"I didn't touch you!" Tosh searched the semi-darkness for Naylor's face.

"Naylor!" he barked, "Keep your bloody hands to yourself I'm warning you!"

"Me? I've had my hands in my pockets since we sat down!"

"One of you is a bloody liar!" said Aisling.

"Not me!" claimed Tosh.

"Me neither!" insisted Naylor.

"Then who the hell is… aargh!" screamed Aisling in a pitch so high she sent the two lads jumping to attention!

"What is it?" asked Tosh as he grabbed her by the arms. Naylor flicked on the torch and flashed it on the table where they had been sitting.

"Jesus!" he roared. "The place is full of rats!"

Like three champion pole-vaulters they leapt up on to the window-ledge and scampered out of the hut.

"Holy mother!" screeched Aisling. "I never got such a fright!"

"Christ, we're only here five minutes and already we've nearly been crushed by an express train and eaten by rats!" laughed Naylor. Tosh and Aisling laughed too, even though all three were breathless with fright.

"Don't tell me you were thick enough to go inside the hut?" the deep husky voice belonged to Sledge, who emerged from behind the hut with his brother Mattie and two other guys. They looked about seventeen but they could very well have been more. Neither Tosh nor Naylor had ever seen them before.

"We thought that was where you wanted to meet us, Sledge!" said Tosh.

"I'd only go in there if I wanted to get a dose of rabies! Sure the place is crawling with rats!" said Sledge who sounded as if he ate gravel three times a day. He pulled out a packet of twenty and offered one to Tosh who shook his head.

"Oh I forgot! You're the super athlete, eh, Tosh!" laughed Sledge mockingly. "Here, Naylor, grab a smoke!"

Naylor never smoked in his life but he was afraid of offending Sledge.

"Thanks, Sledge." He put the cigarette to his lips as Sledge held his lighter to it. He wanted to choke but realised that this was definitely the wrong place to do so. Aisling who had also refused a cigarette giggled as Naylor tried to put on the guise of a forty-a-day man while inside his lungs were screaming for mercy!

"So, Sledge," began Naylor, trying to act cool. "You told me that you had some news for me."

"I do," said Sledge as he inhaled deeply. He blew the smoke out in tiny dense rings and pointed to the two guys standing next to him. "Ringo and Hulk here know a lot more though." They stood mutely for a little while, eyeing each other up and down. Naylor broke the silence.

"So do you know who did the job on my mother?" he asked.

Ringo looked at Hulk who nodded back.

"No, we don't know who did it," he said. Hulk shook his head in agreement.

Naylor was confused. "So what are you doing here for God's sake!"

Again Ringo looked at Hulk who again nodded. Naylor was beginning to wonder whether Hulk was a real person or a giant-sized ventriloquist's dummy!

"We know who called the shots," said Ringo.

Naylor was more confused than ever! "Come again?" he asked shaking his head bewilderedly.

"We know who called the shots... Arranged the job." said Ringo as Hulk continued to nod.

"Who?" asked Naylor. He was getting excited and found himself waving his cigarette into Hulk's face forcing him to speak.

"It's someone you both know very well. He asked us to do

it but we refused. We did jobs for him before but never GBH."

"What in the name of God is GB frigging H?"

"GBH! 'Grievous Bodily Harm'. One step away from manslaughter. No way would we do that!" said Hulk almost proudly. "I mean, collecting debts is okay. We just call around and ask for the cash. If they don't give it we just give them a little threat. But we never mean it. It's just our way of making them pay up faster."

Aisling glared at the two self-confessed loan shark errand boys as if they were a lower life form. Who the hell did they think they were trying to excuse their behaviour in this way? She saw them as a pair of good-for-nothing scumbags. She would have loved to have told them out straight but decided to hold her tongue. They knew something important and this was no time to voice her opinion of them.

"Anyway, we were asked to go to the Heights to collect money from your mam," Ringo took up the story. "We were told that she was going to be used as an example to the rest. He told us to give her a good going over. We said that we weren't interested. No way would we get into that scene. Anyway, when we heard what happened to your mam we wanted to come and tell you for ourselves that it wasn't us."

"So who was it?" asked Naylor.

"We don't know who he got to actually break in and beat her up," said Ringo, "but we want to tell you who the shark is."

"Who?"

"Your football team manager, Gary Quigley."

"Gary!" roared Naylor in disbelief. "You must be joking!"

"No joke," said Ringo. "He's the biggest shark on the northside."

Chapter 14
Gary

Naylor was stunned. Since the attack, he thought of nothing else other than finding out who did it. But now, having been told that Gary Quigley was responsible, he felt totally at a loss. His initial reaction was one of disbelief but as he began to digest the possibility the more it appeared likely.

Gary Quigley was in a perfect position to get to know the people of the Heights. He ran a small bakery off Shandon Street and did his own deliveries in the area. He was on first name terms with several of the residents in or around the Heights.

In his spare time Gary helped out with the local GAA club. Here was another avenue for him to get to know people who might be in need of some extra cash. He was able to call around to the Heights on the pretence of telling the lads about training or games. However, all the time he was gathering information.

"But how could he have two jobs? I mean his bread round would take up a full working week." Naylor was still a little confused.

"I suppose he does his sharking during the hours of darkness!" suggested Tosh.

"Obviously he gets other people to do his dirty work for him. Like Hulk and Ringo," added Aisling.

They were in Naylor's flat that same evening after meeting with Sledge at the Tracks. Aisling had decided that it was time to do some investigating of their own as the garda had told Naylor that they were not following any definite lines of enquiry.

"That's their polite way of telling you that they know damn all!" Tosh told him. They had been on a door-to-door of the Heights but nobody had seen or heard anything. This was not surprising to Tosh and Naylor as silence and a closed mouth was the usual response to a visit from the boys in blue.

"Anyway, Naylor, let's do our own police work!" said Tosh. "Now where does your mam keep her letters and things?"

"In the biscuit tin on top of the cupboard there," pointed Naylor.

Tosh climbed up on a stool and took down the biscuit tin.

" 'Chocolate Coated Kimberley'," he read in a pronounced Sherlock Holmes accent. "What an elaborate filing system the O'Neill family has!"

He giggled as he opened it and threw the contents onto the table. It was a tidy collection of receipts from electricity and other bills. There was no suggestion of a loan of any kind apart from a Credit Union book with receipts dating back since January.

"Nothing out of the ordinary there," explained Naylor. "Me mam saves twenty quid a month for Christmas."

"Is there any other place she keeps things like these?" asked Aisling holding a handful of letters.

Naylor nodded and walked towards a picture of the Sacred Heart which hung from a nail on the kitchen wall. The soft red light flickered softly as he lifted it forwards and put his hand in behind it. He pulled out another neat bundle which was fastened tightly by a thick elastic band.

"These are her private letters. Ones she never wants me to see," he announced almost embarrassedly.

"Yeah," smirked Tosh. "And ones that you always sneak in and read!"

Naylor blushed in agreement and placed the bundle on the table.

"They're nearly all from me dad. She kept them all. He hasn't written for over a year now. I think he's living with someone in Liverpool."

Aisling felt embarrassed looking through the private correspondence and only briefly scanned each letter in case there would be any hint of financial difficulty. There wasn't. She handed her pile back to Naylor who neatly rearranged them all and returned them to the safety of the Sacred Heart's back. Just as he was straightening the picture another envelope slipped to the floor. It wasn't part of the private bundle.

"This looks interesting!" said Naylor as he picked up the letter and scanned the postmark, "Dublin! Who would my mother know in Dublin?"

As he read the letter his hand shook.

"This is it, Tosh."

"What does it say?" asked Aisling.

"'Dear Mrs O'Neill, our agent will be calling in person within ten days with further details of your loan which has been approved.

Amount: £500

Interest: @12% = £60

Period: One Year

Monthly Repayments: £47.66

Method of Repayment: Cash to agent.'"

"Does it name the agent?" asked Aisling.

Naylor scanned the letter then shook his head.

"The name of the company is McGuinness Finance, Westmoreland Street, Dublin 1. They don't say anything about having a Cork office."

"Maybe we could look through the phone book and see if they're listed," suggested Aisling.

"Good idea," said Tosh.

"I'll nip down to the post office. They'll have a phone book there," offered Aisling, knowing that neither Tosh nor Naylor were on the phone.

"No need," said Naylor as he handed her a current directory from the press. "We mightn't have a phone but that doesn't stop us wanting to look up numbers!"

They scanned the phone book for McGuinness Finance. The company had no Cork office. Naylor was quiet for a while as he planned his next move. He could go to the gardai but he was afraid that they wouldn't accept the word of Hulk and Ringo. Besides, Naylor felt they needed more hard evidence. He stared hard at the letter from McGuinness Finance which still lay open on the kitchen table.

"Anybody fancy a trip to the Big Smoke?" he asked.

Chapter 15
Dublin

Cork's Kent Station was buzzing with early morning excitement. It was big match day at Landsdowne Road with Ireland playing England in a European Championship qualifier. Ireland were almost sure of qualification but England had to at least draw to be in with a chance of making the finals in Holland the following year. Hence interest in the game was at fever pitch as swarms of green-clad supporters descended on the station at seven-thirty on that Wednesday morning.

Naylor had wanted to go to Dublin sooner. He wanted to go as soon as he found the letter from McGuinness Finance. However that was on a Friday. There was no point in heading to Dublin that weekend as all the banks and finance houses would be closed until Monday. Tosh persuaded him over the weekend to wait until Wednesday.

"Ireland are playing England. Me dad will get us tickets, no problem. There's a friend of his who drinks in The Bowlers' and he's a selector for the Irish Schoolboys. We can get a note from him for Connolly."

"Yeah! Sure Connolly is soccer crazy. I'll tell her that my dad is bringing me too!" said Aisling.

"I suppose it would look less obvious if the three of us went missing on the day of the match! Sure half the school will be getting off to watch it," added Naylor who was beginning to come around to their way of thinking.

Miss Connolly accepted their excuses without question. A huge queue paraded in conveyor belt fashion in and out of the office. She nodded and smiled as each note seeking permission to join the Green Army was held up for her approval.

"Let's hope the boys in Green do the business!" she smiled at each of them as the queue moved swiftly along.

"There he is!" announced Tosh as he spotted his uncle Tim coming into the station hall and heading towards the platform. Tim was a train steward and had promised Tosh a free ride on the train.

"Three of you?" moaned Tim.

"Sorry Uncle Tim but I forgot to mention Aisling. You don't mind do you?" Tosh apologised but he knew that Tim wouldn't be a problem. He was a grumpy old sod who loved to complain but Tosh knew he wouldn't leave them down.

"Of course I bloody well mind! I'm putting me job on the line here Tosh! If an inspector finds out I'd be out on me ear and I have only another six months to go before me pension!" Uncle Tim was complaining already!

"Sorry Uncle Tim. But we'll make sure we're not caught!" promised Tosh. "Just tell us where to go and we'll do exactly as you say."

"Okay. Follow me. There's a freight carriage on this train taking crates of pottery. Go in there. It won't be emptied until the train gets to Dublin. I'll try to get to the carriage before the porter opens the doors. For God's sake don't come out from behind the crates until I tell you or you'll give the poor chap a heart attack!"

Tim was feeling very important now as he led them to the carriage. He looked all around him before he ushered them inside and whispered to them to keep the noise down. Then he slammed the doors closed. Suddenly they found themselves in total darkness.

The journey to Dublin was a magical experience which Tosh hoped would last forever. He was sitting next to Aisling. Naylor seemed to be content to sit with his own thoughts at the far end of the carriage which suited Tosh down to the ground. He wanted Aisling's company all to himself. For the past week it had always been a question of the three of them and Tosh was beginning to feel like telling Naylor to go take a hike. Anytime he suggested to Aisling that they would go for a walk Naylor would offer to come along too. However on the train Tosh found himself next to Aisling sitting on the floor behind two huge freight crates.

The delicious smell of roses teased his nostrils. He prayed that this train would crawl all the way to Dublin. They spoke in whispers which made Tosh feel warm inside. He tried to pluck up the courage to put his arm around her but he was terrified that she would ask him to take it away again. Then they'd both be embarrassed and the warm feeling he was enjoying would disappear in the awkward silence of the remaining miles to Dublin. For now he would just be content with the whispers, the warmth and the rose fragrance.

After about two hours of wondering whether he should or he shouldn't, Aisling put her hand on his to emphasise a point she was making. Tosh didn't know whether it was his own reflex action or hers but his fingers opened and she slipped her hand into his. In the semi-darkness they smiled at each other and to Tosh's delight she didn't take her hand away. Tosh hoped that the train would stop in every village and town from there to Dublin!

Unfortunately for Tosh the train stopped only at Mallow and Limerick Junction and was in Dublin in two and a half hours. It was only when the train screeched to a halt in Heuston Station that they realised they were back in civilisation. The happy choruses of "Ole! Ole! Ole!" could be clearly heard in the freight carriage as they sat on the floor surrounded by crates of pottery. It may have been this sudden awakening that caused Tosh to make the mistake against which he had been warned earlier.

As the carriage door was wrenched open he sprang to his feet and leaped forward like a lion released from a cage.

"Jesus, Mary and Joseph!" roared the astonished station guard. "It's a hold-up!"

The poor man was convinced that he had uncovered the next great train robbery. He blew hard on his whistle several times. Tosh tried to explain to him that he was, at worst, a stowaway and that robbing crates of pottery was really not his style. But it was no use.

"Just stay away from me!" screamed the guard in between more frantic blows on the whistle.

"Would you stop blowing that thing for God's sake! You'll have the police here!"

Tosh tried to restrain him from blowing the whistle but this only made matters worse.

"What's the matter?" asked Naylor who emerged from behind a large crate to find Tosh and the station guard wrestling with the whistle.

"There's two of them!" roared the guard who was now hysterical.

A large crowd began to gather as two gardai ran up the platform to investigate. They had been on special match day duty. The last thing they expected was to be called to a train hold-up.

One of the gardai held Tosh in a head lock with both arms twisted high up on his back. The other cautioned Naylor and Aisling who were still in the carriage.

"Just step down slowly with your hands on your heads!"

Naylor was reminded of a scene from a wild west movie as he played the role of the baddie moving slowly to the awaiting sheriff. However as he felt the handcuffs cut against his wrists he realised that this was no bit part in a B-movie.

"For crying out loud, let them go! Can't you see they're only a couple of kids?"

It was Uncle Tim playing the part of Clint Eastwood who was stepping in to save the day. When he heard the whistle he knew straight away what had happened. He tried to get to the scene before the gardai but he was distracted by some businessman demanding an apology for his having to stand all the way from Limerick Junction.

"It's my fault guards!" announced Tim. "I saw this young girl crying at Cork Station. Some pickpocket had stolen her purse with her train tickets and match tickets. I know I shouldn't have had, but I put them in the freight carriage. I'm sorry if I gave you a fright, Dinny, but I hadn't a chance to warn you before you opened the doors!"

The gardai immediately released the three as Tim continued to apologise and hoped that Tosh had the sense not to call him Uncle Tim.

"So, you have no tickets for the game at Landsdowne?" asked the taller of the two gardai who had been holding Tosh in the head lock.

"Er... no!" said Naylor playing along with Tim's sad tale with a nobody's child look on his face!

"Everything is gone!" said Aisling who hoped that the guards wouldn't want to look into her shoulder bag in which she kept her purse and their precious match tickets!

"We thought we'd come up anyway and try to pick up some tickets outside the stadium," she added, not realising how much fun she was having lying to the guards.

The taller guard put his hand inside his jacket and pulled out a bundle of tickets. He handed three of them to Aisling.

"Here you go!" he said. "I just confiscated these from a tout outside the station ten minutes ago! Enjoy the game. We'll be here afterwards and we'll make sure you'll get on the train home."

Tosh began to shake with excitement! Three upper stand tickets! They were worth twenty-five quid a piece! These were even better than the tickets his dad had got them! There was no time to lose. If they were to get into Dublin and find McGuinness Finance before the game they would have to start moving.

"Thanks a million! These are brilliant!" Tosh smiled at Dinny the porter who still looked as if he had gone twelve rounds with a serial killer. "Sorry about the mix-up, sir, oh, and here's your whistle back!"

As the three of them made their way up the platform to the bus stop, Tosh glanced over his shoulder and winked at Tim who just hoped the gardai hadn't noticed.

"Jesus Tosh you are one frigging eejit! We could all have ended up in a cell for the night!" said Naylor as the bus crawled up past the Liffey, en route to O'Connell Bridge. Tosh grinned back at him and mischievously waved the tickets under his nose!

"Olé! Olé! Olé!" he smirked joining in the sing-song which was already in full swing on the bus!

"First things first," Naylor reminded him. "We must find this McGuinness Finance place."

Chapter 16
Finding Out

Once on O'Connell Bridge it didn't take them long to find their bearings. Aisling had been to Dublin several times and knew that Westmoreland Street led to the Trinity College and Grafton Street area. As the match crowd made their way to the Tara Street DART station or to the various city centre pubs and restaurants, Aisling led Tosh and Naylor across Burgh Quay and up along Westmoreland Street.

"I've never seen such traffic!" said Tosh. "It's more like Tokyo than Dublin!"

"It's chaotic today. It always is on match days," explained Aisling.

"It's over there!" announced Naylor. "Over that pub on the third floor!"

Aisling and Tosh strained their eyes to read the lettering on the third floor window.

"You're right, Naylor. How in the name of God did you read that? You're supposed to be half blind!" laughed Tosh.

Aisling laughed too but Naylor just looked straight ahead as he crossed the road. It wasn't that he was offended by Tosh's remarks. Far from it. Tosh and himself were constantly passing wisecracks about each other. His eyesight was a favourite topic of fun. At this moment however he wasn't interested in playful banter with Tosh. He was concentrating on how he was going to find out all he could from McGuinness Finance.

"Now listen, when we go in let me do all the talking. You just play along with what I'm saying. We're from the community school in Clontarf and we're on an assignment."

"Is there a community school in Clontarf?" asked Aisling.

"I've no idea," said Naylor, "but it doesn't matter."

"It might bloody well matter if the receptionist is from Clontarf!" suggested Aisling who wasn't too happy with the plan so far.

"Look! Just let me do the talking okay!" Naylor was putting his foot down. This was his plan and he wasn't going to let it fail.

They climbed the two flights of stairs and pushed open the glass doors. Inside, the office was air-conditioned and neon-lit. Behind a desk sat a man in his early twenties who was half eyeing them and half answering the telephone. He pointed to a large sofa indicating that they should wait until he had finished the call. This pleased Naylor who scanned the office with the precision of a seasoned detective. He made a mental note of all the office equipment. He was relieved to discover that they were using an IBM computer system. He had used an IBM in school.

When he had taken his call and typed something into his computer the receptionist called them to his desk.

"Well, lads! How can I help you?"

"Were you not expecting us?" asked Naylor in a Dublin accent as broad as any you might hear in Moore Street.

"Mm... not unless you have an appointment. I'll just check the appointment schedule. Your name?"

"We're from Clontarf Community... Our principal, Mrs Sisk, made the arrangements." The young man typed in a code on the computer on his desk. A list of names and times flashed on the screen.

"Ah, yes, Mrs Sisk is timed for an eleven-thirty appointment." Aisling and Tosh couldn't believe their ears. How did Naylor know that Mrs Sisk had an appointment at eleven-thirty? Who was Mrs Sisk? Naylor obviously had all this worked out in advance

"Well the appointment was made by Mrs Sisk but it is actually for us. She probably was too busy to explain over the phone but that's no problem because I'm used to explaining this. It happens all the time! You see we're in transition year because we're too young to sit for the Leaving Cert. We're doing a project on technological changes in Irish business and industry. Basically we go to a different place of work each week and write up a report afterwards. We just want to find out how you keep data filed, use of fax machines, modems, word processing and that sort of thing. I have a questionnaire prepared if you'd just give me five minutes of your time!"

"Sounds great!" The young man was impressed. "Hang on I'll get us some coffee before we start. He picked up the in house phone and ordered four coffees. He then picked up another phone and spoke to his boss who instantly emerged from her office. She looked more like a film star than a financial executive.

"Good morning," she smiled at them, "Welcome to McGuinness Finance. I'm Ann Marie McGuinness, Managing Director. I'm delighted you chose us as part of your project. Ciarán here is my secretary. He's my right-hand man! He'll tell you all you need to know and maybe show you around later. You must send us a copy of your report when you've finished it. It sounds like a great idea!"

Naylor momentarily forgot why he was there as he fell in love with Ann Marie McGuinness. He had never imagined that a managing director could look so gorgeous. She was about thirty with wavy black hair, a beautiful figure and a smile that wouldn't look out of place on a toothpaste commercial. He made a mental note to become a personal secretary when he left school. When he had recovered he stood up and shook her extended hand.

"Thanks very much, Miss McGuinness. I'll post you a copy within the next few weeks!" he lied.

The coffee arrived and was placed on Ciarán's desk. Naylor pulled out the questionnaire and quickly recorded Ciarán's answers.

"Number of employees in head office?"

"Twelve, including Miss McGuinness."

"How long in operation?"

"Nine years."

"Nature of business?"

"Provision of financial services."

"Could you be more specific?"

"Sure! We provide financial advice to people who request it.

Advice on anything to do with investing money, inheritances, pension schemes or getting loans."

"So you're also a lending agency?"

"That would be part of our brief, yes."

"Fine," said Naylor as he wrote down Ciarán's comments verbatim.

"Any sub-offices around the country?"

"No, but we have regional agents in most areas. They work from home and are linked up by computer to us."

"Would these be full-time agents?"

"Mainly full-time yes. But in some more densely populated areas such as Dublin, Cork, Limerick, Waterford City, we employ part-time staff as well. They work in conjunction with our full-time agents."

Naylor had cracked it. It was beginning to make sense. Gary was obviously one of these part-time agents.

Naylor moved on to the technology questions. He had prepared the questionnaire the week before at school. On the same day he had also phoned McGuinness Finance and made the eleven-thirty appointment for the fictious head teacher of Clontarf Community School, Mrs Sisk!

Ciarán was totally convinced by the whole charade, as were Aisling and Tosh. Aisling was beginning to believe that she really was in transition year in Clontarf Community School!

Tosh was lost when Ciarán explained the computer system. Naylor jotted down his responses with a knowing air.

"Would you like to see how the system works?" asked Ciarán.

"Sure. We'd love to." Naylor was hoping to look around on his own but Ciarán seemed too enthusiastic in his role as host to let him wander freely.

"Just say for example that I wanted to pass on information to our agent in Galway. I could fax him a message. But I could also pass the information directly on to his computer. When he turns on his computer and types MESSAGES, my message will appear on the screen."

"And I suppose it works both ways," said Aisling.

"Of course. All any of our agents has to do is to type in reports or accounts and enter it into the network and we have the information on disk instantly."

"That's incredible!" said Naylor who knew all about the system but was pretending to hear about it for the first time. If only he could get five minutes to play around with it he could find the information he needed. Just as he was feeling he was losing his chance Miss McGuinness came to the door and called Ciarán.

"I'll be right back!" he told them.

"Take your time!" Naylor told him, and he meant every word.

When the office door closed Naylor sprang into action. He selected the database and typed in AGENTS. A list appeared on the screen. He read through them. There was no sign of Gary's name. He typed CORK. This time a menu appeared on the screen. He selected LOANS and another list flashed before his eyes. He saw his mother's name on the screen. He selected it from the list and pressed the RETURN button. An account sheet similar to the one he had found in the kitchen behind the picture of the Sacred Heart appeared on the screen. Mrs O'Neill had borrowed five hundred pounds at twelve per cent with monthly repayments over one year of forty-seven pounds sixty-seven pence. At the end of the screen there was a date after which were the words ACCOUNT SETTLED.

"Naylor!" said Tosh excitedly. "Your mam has paid her debt!"

"Hurry, Naylor! That Ciarán guy might be back any moment!" whispered Aisling but Naylor was engrossed.

"She may have paid her debt to McGuinness Finance. But look at the name of the sub-agent at the top right-hand corner of the screen."

"Pádraig G Ó Coigligh," read Aisling out loud. "What's that in English?"

"Patrick G Quigley," said Naylor. "The G is for Gearóid, or Gary as he likes to be called! It's a safe bet that me mam has been taking top up loans from him on the side."

Naylor memorised the code for Pádraig G Ó Coigligh and

decided to send him a quick message through the network.

"Naylor! What are you doing?" asked Aisling anxiously. "He'll be back any minute!"

"Ssh! This won't take long," Naylor assured her as he typed speedily.

"CALL TO MISS O'FARRELL, 13 MCGILLICUDDY HEIGHTS. THURSDAY, 3 MARCH. 6 pm re: PERSONAL LOAN."

"Who is this Miss O'Farrell?" asked Aisling.

Tosh was finding it difficult to contain his laughter. "She's sort of a neighbour of ours! Quick, Naylor, your man is coming back!"

Naylor jotted down more numbers from the screen on the back of the questionnaire before turning off the computer and clearing the screen. Deftly he switched it on again and keyed in the file which was initially on the screen. Without a second to spare Ciarán returned. He apologised for leaving them for so long.

"That's fine," said Naylor. "Listen, you've been a great help. I'll send you a copy of our project when we've typed it up. Thanks for everything!"

When they were back out on Westmoreland Street Tosh patted Naylor on the back.

"Naylor, that was outstanding! You were brilliant in there. And that message you sent about Miss O'Farrell and the loan was a master stroke! Pure bloody genius!"

Aisling however was not amused.

"I don't think that was a very nice thing to do, Naylor. That poor neighbour of yours is going to have Gary around pestering her to take out a loan!"

"I doubt it!" said Naylor grinning.

"But you sent him the message to call on her tomorrow night."

"If he manages to get her to take out a loan then he'll be the greatest salesman of all time!" said Tosh.

"How come?" asked Aisling who sounded confused.

"Miss O'Farrell died four months ago!"

Chapter 17

Olé! Olé! Olé!

Going to the match was a welcome relief. The past ten days had been exhausting for each of the three of them. Aisling was feeling a lot better about her father but she was still upset that her mother and her brothers were still in France. She had spoken on the phone to her mother the night before and had tried to explain that things had changed.

"Dad is a different person, Mum, honestly. He is really being so nice. He cooks breakfast every morning and dinner is always ready after school. He keeps saying how sorry he is for making everybody so miserable."

Aisling could sense that her mother wasn't totally surprised to hear this. She too had noticed a change in her husband from his frequent telephone calls to France. However, she wasn't convinced that rushing home just because he seemed to be in better humour would solve anything at the moment.

"Let's just see how things go over the next few weeks, Aisling. Let's see how long he can keep it up," she told her.

Aisling was sure that things could only improve. Her father had been so much more cheerful since the evening they had discussed his redundancy. Although he still complained about being out of work, he had applied for jobs from the paper and had even contacted the university for details of courses. He quite liked the idea of becoming a student.

"I might wait until you have the Leaving Cert done and we could go there together!" he told her jokingly. If only Mum could see him like this, she thought.

They were sitting in Burger King at lunch time. There was a big match special offer of a "Bacon Double Cheese Burger with Large Fries and Mineral" which they each tucked into. They ate in silence as the excitement of their early morning adventures yielded to hunger.

Naylor welcomed the absence of conversation. All around them both English and Irish supporters sat in noisy groups singing and chanting at each other. Naylor seemed oblivious to it all. He was filled with a sense of satisfaction. He had tracked Gary down. He knew now how he operated. It was no longer a hunch but a fact. Gary was a part-time agent for McGuinness Finance. McGuinness Finance operated legitimately. As far as they were concerned Betty O'Neill had taken out a loan and paid it back. What they didn't know was that their part-time agent in the Cork area was organising his own loans. Gary the loan shark. Naylor had enough information on him now to go to the gardai. However, he just wanted to apply his own piece of justice first.

"Come on you two, eat up! We've got to be in our seats before two-thirty. We can catch the DART from over the bridge there." Tosh was on top of the world. He had really enjoyed himself this morning. Even nearly getting arrested had proved profitable. Being with Aisling had been the highlight though. He couldn't help feeling giddy inside at the thought of holding her hand and sitting so close to her in the freight carriage. He was half sorry that the gardai had told them that they would fix them up with seats for the return train. Sitting in an air-conditioned no smoking carriage hadn't a fraction of the romance of travelling by freight! Still, the day was young yet and there was a little score to be settled at Landsdowne Road.

The match was a classic. It was real blood and guts stuff! England were winning all the way through after Ireland gave away a penalty in the first minute. Tosh, Aisling and Naylor could barely watch as the minutes ticked away and an English victory was on the cards. Their seats were first class. They were in the front row of the top tier above the halfway line. They were surrounded by famous faces from the world of sport and television. It was like an A to Z of celebrities! Tosh couldn't wait to go home and tell his dad. On the way up to their seats they bumped into Gary Lineker who was on his way to the press box to cover the game for

BBC Radio Five.

"Gary, would you sign this for me dad? He thinks you were the best ever... besides Niall Quinn, that is!"

"And Paul McGrath!" added Naylor.

"And John Giles!" said Aisling.

"I suppose fourth best isn't too bad!" smiled the former Spurs and England star as he signed his name on each of their match programmes.

Tosh kept looking at the autograph all through the match. "To Ger Twomey, Up The Boys In Green! Regards, Gary Lineker." His dad would get some reaction in The Bowlers' when he would show them all that one!

With seconds to go, and with things looking perfect for Gary Lineker and the rest of the English contingent, there was a mighty roar from the Landsdowne crowd. A free kick from the right of the centre circle landed in the penalty area. There was a frantic scramble and suddenly the ball was in the England net!

"Yeeeeesssssss!"

"We did it!"

"Olé! Olé! Olé! Olé! Olé! Olé!"

Everybody was dancing around the place hugging and kissing. Aisling threw her arms around Tosh while Naylor stood up on his seat and kissed a perfect stranger who was wearing a red, white and blue scarf! She wasn't too impressed!

"Sod off, Paddy!" she told him but Naylor was beyond caring. Under normal circumstances he would have taken this as a racial slur! But this was different! Call me what you like he thought, this is pure magic! He continued to dance on his feet chanting Olé! Olé! Olé! with the other forty thousand Irish supporters in the stadium. They were hoarse from singing "You'll Never Beat The Irish!"

When the final whistle blew they were still singing. The English were singing too as both teams had qualified for Holland. Landsdowne Road had never seen anything like it! Every face expressed utter joy as strangers embraced strangers!

"Sorry about that a while ago, mate!" offered Naylor's English friend who had earlier insulted him.

"No problem! But you're not getting another kiss!" Naylor told her.

The three wrapped their arms around each other and skipped their way to the DART. They sang all the way back into Dublin.

At Heuston Station the two gardai were waiting for them. They bypassed the long queue for the six o'clock to Cork as they were led up the platform and on to the train. Exhausted, they sat back into their seats and watched the delighted home-bound fans swarm on to the train to join them. Tosh sat next to Naylor with Aisling facing them both. Suddenly Tosh sat bolt upright.

"Naylor!"

"What?" Naylor had taken off his glasses and was drifting off to sleep.

"Put on your specs fast!"

Naylor nearly exploded when he saw them! At the far end of the platform they stood gazing into each others eyes lovingly. Suddenly they plunged into a long kiss. Then she backed away and waved, blowing him more kisses as he made his way along the platform to join the queue for the Cork train. Pádraig G Ó Coigligh had just said goodbye to Miss Ann Marie McGuinness!

Chapter 18
Preparations

"Do you think she knows what he's doing in Cork?" asked Tosh.

"No way!" said Naylor.

"Come on, Naylor," said Tosh. "You're just defending her because you think she's a fine thing!"

"Cut it out, Tosh!" snapped Naylor, who was annoyed that Tosh could read his mind at times.

"There is no doubt that Miss Ann Marie McGuinness is a beautiful looking woman," stated Naylor, matter-of-factly. "However, that has got nothing whatsoever to do with my judgement of her."

"Oh no?" laughed Tosh.

"I think that if she knew what Gary was up to she would drop him like a hot spud!"

"Why do you say that?"

"She doesn't have to get involved with loan sharking. Did you not see the network she operates? She is the managing director of a very successful financial institution. She would be out of her tiny mind if she would risk all that by messing around with loan sharks!"

"So do we ring her and tell her?" asked Tosh who relished the thought of spilling the beans on Gary. He hoped Naylor would say yes and allow him to do the talking!

"All in good time, Tosh," said Naylor. "Very soon it won't be just Miss McGuinness who will be finding out the truth about our Mr Quigley!"

"I can't wait!"

"Me neither. Come on, let's get some sleep. Tomorrow is D-day."

The two lads had spent hours whispering in their bunk beds. Tosh drifted off easily dreaming of Aisling, crates of pottery and soft hands. Naylor found sleeping difficult. It had been an incredible day. Spotting Gary in the station with

Miss McGuinness had freaked him out. However it did explain how Gary happened to be working for McGuinness Finance in the first place. He was relieved when Gary was unable to get on their train. It was full and he was forced to wait for a later one. It would have been almost impossible trying to avoid him had he managed to get on board. They'd have spent the entire journey wishing they were travelling in the freight carriage.

Eventually he drifted into a fitful sleep. Images flashed through his mind of his mother, of Gary, of Hulk and Ringo, of Ann Marie McGuinness and Landsdowne Road. The sounds of computers, whistles and trains and "Come on you boys in green!" whirled around in his head. He tossed and turned as these images and sounds gradually gelled into a seemingly endless nightmare in which he was being chased by a train. Both his feet were stuck to the tracks. As the train came nearer he saw Gary's face in Thomas The Tank Engine-fashion snarling at him! His feet became even more immobile as Gary The Tank Engine growled and hissed and threatened a nasty, painful death.

He awoke just in time to avoid that horrific final moment. His head was spinning. His heart raced with palpitations and his forehead was dotted with beads of cold sweat. He lay on his bunk and listened to Tosh snoring above him. Normally he would have thrown a pillow at him and let out a string of curses until Tosh would eventually turn on his side and stop snoring. However, in the darkness of pre-dawn, he felt reassured to hear the sound of his friend sleeping above him. Soon he became aware of the early morning city-bound traffic as it steadily increased. He must have drifted into a snooze for a few minutes as when the radio alarm went off it woke him with a start.

"Turn that frigging thing off, Naylor!" moaned Tosh.

That was always Tosh's way of saying good morning. The clock was always set for seven which gave them an extra twenty minutes to lie on. Naylor reached over and pushed the OFF button. His whole body felt drained. This was definitely one of those no-school-today days.

Besides his exhaustion there were other reasons why Naylor needed to stay away from school. He had things to organise. He asked Tosh to tell Miss Connolly that he had to meet his social worker. This was partly the truth. Tosh's father was expecting a visit from the social worker that morning. Naylor's mother wouldn't be out of hospital for another two to three weeks, so the Southern Health Board wanted Ger Twomey to sign a custodial form to cover that period. In short he would act as guardian to Naylor in the absence of Mrs O'Neill. There was in fact no need for Naylor to be there at all but he convinced Mr Twomey that he should be present.

"I just want to be sure they don't try to foster me out when me back is turned!" he told Mr Twomey from the breakfast table as he force-fed himself a bowl of porridge.

"If they wanted to foster you out, Naylor, they would just go ahead and do it with or without your being here. But if it makes you feel any better you can stay." Mr Twomey told him. He liked Naylor and he knew that he had been on edge of late. He figured it was to do with his mother so he was anxious to keep him happy at all costs.

There was a long pause as Tosh raced through his flakes and Naylor was grateful that Ger Twomey wasn't forcing him to go to school. Ger sat on a stool at the worktop reading and enjoying a cup of tea.

"That Gary is some man!" he suddenly proclaimed.

"What!" roared both Tosh and Naylor in disbelief. What in the name of God did Ger Twomey know about Gary?

Ger gave them a bewildered look as he pointed to his reading material. Neither of them had noticed that he was reading the match programme with the personal message Tosh had got signed.

"Gary Lineker! What a player he was! Pure genius! I can't wait to show this to the boys in The Bowlers' tonight!"

The two boys sighed deeply and finished their breakfasts

in a state of relieved silence.

As it turned out there was no question of Naylor being fostered. The social worker was in the flat for less than two minutes. She was businesslike and to the point. She briefly explained what was involved and handed Ger a form to read and sign. When Ger Twomey put his name on the dotted line he was *in loco parentis* until Mrs O'Neill was well enough to come home.

"You might as well head off to school now, Tony. It's still early enough!" Ger told Naylor, as he played Daddy to him for the first time officially. "I'll give you a note if you want one."

"It's okay, Mr Twomey. I'll do a bit of studying on my own later on. It would be half-ten before I'd get there at this stage and I've already missed double maths."

Naylor felt a little guilty lying to Ger Twomey. Neither Tosh nor himself had told him anything about Gary. He would have insisted on going to the gardai straight away. Tosh and Aisling had both tried to persuade Naylor on the train ride home that he had done enough but Naylor wasn't ready to hand over to the boys in blue yet.

As soon as Ger closed the door behind him before starting his morning walk, Naylor sprang into action. There were people to see and things to be done.

When Tosh arrived at the flat after school Naylor was just in the door before him.

"Have you got it?" asked Naylor.

"Yeah."

"It doesn't make much noise, does it?"

"No, it records silently!" Tosh told him "Aisling showed me how to use it. It's dead cool!"

"Brilliant, but we better bring the tape recorder as well just in case something goes wrong. Will you manage both, Tosh?"

"No bother!"

"Right off you go so, Tosh. The others are expecting you at

about quarter past five. It shouldn't take that long to get ready. Does Aisling know where the flat is?"

"Yeah I told her first floor, turn left at the top of the stairs and it's number thirteen. She said she'd be there at about twenty-to."

"Okay! Go for it, Tosh! I'll see you back here at eight. For God's sake be careful!"

"You too, Naylor. See you, boy!"

Chapter 19

Introducing Caroline

Miss O'Farrell had lived alone in the Heights since they were built. On her death the flat became the property of Cork Corporation and had remained unoccupied. It was used as a place to hang out by the local kids. Miss O'Farrell had no family therefore nobody had bothered to come to collect her furniture. It suited the Corporation to leave it that way as it gave the impression that the flat was occupied. This, they thought, would reduce the threat of a break-in. However, nothing could have been further from the truth. Every night there was some party or other in Miss O'Farrells! Sledge had managed to get keys cut and charged for their use.

Sledge hadn't been surprised when Naylor had come to see him earlier that day. Ever since the incident in the laneway, when Naylor had made him wish he had worn armour-plated underpants, he realised that Naylor's puny appearance was deceptive. Naylor was a fighter. He was determined to do things his way.

"Just make sure that there are no kids around Miss O'Farrell's at six!"

"No problem, Naylor!" croaked Sledge. "Here, have a fag!"

"No thanks Sledge. I've quit!"

"Quit? How many did you smoke?"

"One."

"One a day?"

"No. Just one ever. That day up here when you introduced me to your animal friends."

"Hulk and Ringo?"

"Yeah!"

"Hulk and Ringo are okay when you get to know them."

"I'm sure they must be," said Naylor without conviction. "Anyway, Sledge, can I have the keys?"

"Sure, Naylor, here you go," Sledge handed him two front

door keys to Miss O'Farrell's.

"Are you sure she'll be able to do it?" asked Naylor.

"Of course I'm sure. She always got the lead part in school plays. She's brilliant, I'm telling you."

"But does she look old enough? I mean, she's only nineteen."

"Listen, Naylor boy. We went to see her in a pantomime at the Everyman when she was Old Mother Hubbard. She was only ten then and I was convinced I was looking at me nan on the stage!"

Sledge was enthusing about his sister Caroline who had earlier that morning agreed to help out. Naylor knew he couldn't do it without a woman pretending to be Miss O'Farrell. He had thought of Aisling but she would look too young even with make-up. Caroline was Sledge's suggestion. She wasn't a bit like her brothers. She was sane! She was studying for a BA at UCC but spent most of her time acting with Dramat, the drama society there.

"This will be great!" she told Naylor. "I can make up the lines as I go along!"

"Not quite!" Naylor warned, "I want you to get him to say all the right things!"

"You mean all the wrong things!" came the frog-like wisecrack from Sledge.

They met again up on the Tracks later that day when Sledge handed over the keys and Naylor admitted he was a non-smoker.

"You should give them up yourself some time, Sledge!"

"First things first, Naylor. I haven't had a drop of cider for a week and I don't think any of us will go near glue again after what happened to... Axle." Sledge looked away. Mentioning Axle's name was painful to him. He sniffed deeply in an effort to control the tears. There was an embarrassed pause as Sledge rubbed his cheeks with the back of his hands. The hard man was softening. Naylor tried not to notice.

"Sorry, Naylor!" said Sledge when he was eventually able to speak again.

"That's okay, Sledge. Thanks for the keys."

"No problem! I'll be there at about quarter-past with Caroline. I'll hang around afterwards to make sure you're not disturbed. Good luck, Naylor."

Chapter 20

Good Evening Miss O'Farrell

Tosh sat hunched in the kitchen. The hole he had bored in the wall was just large enough for him to see into the living-room without being noticed. It was six o'clock exactly when the doorbell rang. If Gary was nothing else he was punctual.

"Hello!" Gary's voice rattled with friendliness, "I've come to see Miss O'Farrell. Is she at home?"

"What do you want her for?" Aisling's soft accent had disappeared as she barked at Gary.

"I'm from McGuinness Finance. Here's my card. She asked me to call for an appointment."

"You'd better come in and wait."

Tosh watched Gary come in and sit down. He dressed like an executive in a smart double-breasted suit and and a dazzling hand-printed tie. Prat! he whispered to himself. He saw Gary eyeing Aisling up and down. Aisling had deliberately tarted herself up. Caked in make-up she looked about seventeen. She wore a mini skirt up to her waist and a low cut, tight-fitting tee-shirt.

"So, is your mother here?" asked Gary after a minute or two of silence.

"She'll be back soon," Aisling sat down alongside him on the couch making him feel very uncomfortable.

"I love the suit!" she said as she softly ran her hand up the sleeve.

"Thanks!" He replied awkwardly pulling his arm away. "Mm... do you go to school locally?" He asked in an effort to make reasonable conversation.

"No. I don't go at all. I was asked to leave in fifth year!" Her hand was back on his arm stroking it teasingly.

"Oh... Why was that?"

Aisling leaned over to him so that her face was level and almost touching his.

"Because I had an affair with my class teacher!" She licked

her lips wickedly and moved even closer to kiss him.

Gary gulped and tried to get up. Tosh nearly exploded! What in the name of God was Aisling playing at? If Naylor had anything to do with this part of the plan he promised to twist his neck. Just as Aisling threw her arms around Gary and was about to start smothering him with kisses the front door burst open! Caroline was bang on cue!

"Get your filthy paws off her, you dirty animal!" Caroline's voice was so like that of the late and much-lamented Miss O'Farrell that for a split second Tosh thought she had resurrected herself for the occasion.

"Good evening, Mrs O'Farrell!" muttered Gary in confusion as he tried to pull himself together.

"Miss!" snarled Caroline. "And who in the name of God Almighty and His Blessed Mother are you?"

"Pádraig Ó Coigligh... McGuinness Finance. You asked for an appointment to discuss loan arrangements."

"I know I bloody well did. But I certainly did not ask you to come around and slobber all over me one and only daughter!"

"Mm... I think you've got hold of the wrong end of the stick here... "

"I think it's you who has a problem holding on to things, me boy!"

Gary tried hard to come up with an explanation. He blushed and stammered as he tried to gain control of the situation. Caroline was enjoying herself. Aisling too was playing a blinder. However she didn't want to frighten him away.

"I was only trying to fix his tie, Mam.... and I slipped!"

"Oh yeah?"

"Honestly!"

"You just mind yourself, young lady! We had enough trouble with you last year in school when the nuns sent for me. Merciful God! I was never so embarrassed in me whole life!" She paused for effect and turned her attention from Aisling to Gary who wasn't quite sure whether to sit, stand or simply make a run for it!

"Now young fella!" Caroline stared at him. "What did you say your name was?"

"Pádraig Ó Coigligh... from McGuinness Finance!" For the first time since he came into the flat Gary began to relax a little. He decided to seize the moment and get straight down to business.

"Now, Miss O'Farrell. How much of a loan were you looking for?"

"Six hundred pounds!"

Gary jotted down the figure. "I see. And what income do you have?"

"Just me single mother's allowance and the children's allowance for Sally Ann there!"

Aisling smiled as Gary glanced at her. She picked the name Sally Ann herself when she and Caroline had planned their strategy.

"So Sally Ann is still of school-going age."

"Yes. Sure she's only fourteen!"

Gary swallowed hard and cleared his throat. Expelled from fifth year, my backside, he thought to himself. Aisling saw him looking at her and blew him a kiss. Gary turned his eyes away from her and switched his attention back to matters financial.

He put down his pen and paused for a moment as if he was going to explain something very profound.

"Miss O'Farrell. I am very sorry to have wasted your time but I'm afraid McGuinness Finance are unable to give you a loan. Your means of support are limited to say the least. It would be against company policy to sanction any loan for you"

"But I need the money. Me sister's son is getting married in England next month and I promised her that meself and Sally Ann would be over."

Gary stared hard and paused again. Then he looked over his shoulder as if he was making sure nobody was listening from behind.

"Mm... There is, of course, one other way."

"What's that?"

"I could arrange the loan privately through my own company."

Tosh's hand began to shake as he focused the camera on Gary's face. Gotcha!

"I don't understand!" Caroline tried to sound confused and was doing brilliantly!

"You see I deal with lots of clients who can never get a bank loan. Therefore I give them a private loan which they can pay me back over a set time. We'll say in your case eighteen months at roughly forty-five pounds per month."

"You're not a loan shark, are you?" Caroline knew she was on thin ice but she felt that this would be exactly what the woman whom she was pretending to be would have asked.

"Not at all!" laughed Gary as he tried to make his lie credible, "No no! I'm simply providing a service which my company and other banks could never provide. I would ask you, of course, to be discreet about this. McGuinness Finance would take a very poor view of my going against company policy."

"You mean it's illegal!" Caroline pretended to sound shocked.

"No, of course it's not illegal. I'm merely helping you to get over a difficult time and you can pay me back at your convenience. It's just that it would be better if we kept this to ourselves. Let's call it a private agreement and as such no-one else need know anything about it. Mum's the word, and all that!"

"Okay so! How soon can I have the money?"

"I can bring it to you tomorrow. Now, I do need some security."

"What do you mean security?" asked Caroline who had guessed what was coming next.

"In the unlikely event that you should fail to pay me on time I need to protect my investment. I want you to give me your social security book. I'll give it back to you on the evening before payment day so you can draw your money and pay me what you owe on time. I do have an unwritten rule that if you miss a payment then an extra monthly amount is added on as a penalty!"

"That sounds harsh!" said Caroline.

"Well I'm only covering myself. If you pay up on time there will be no need for any penalty. After all I'm the one putting the money up front."

Caroline stood up and walked around the room. She gave the impression that she was considering his proposal. Suddenly she turned and faced him.

"Cash!" she insisted.

"Of course, Miss O'Farrell!"

"Call around tomorrow at twelve. I agree to your terms. Do I have to sign anything?"

"Not at all. Just get me your social security book and I'll be on my way. I wouldn't want to keep Sally Ann away from her homework any longer!"

"That's very considerate of you... honey!" smirked Aisling who flashed her eyes and mouthed Gary another kiss. She was enjoying her flirtatious role even more now that she knew Gary had walked right into their trap.

"I wasn't born yesterday boy! You'll get my social security book when I get me six hundred pounds!" barked Caroline.

"Very well. I'll see you in the morning, Miss O'Farrell. Thank you for your time. I'll see myself out!"

After he had left the flat Caroline and Aisling counted to ten before leaving out a whoop of sheer delight. Tosh emerged from the kitchen waving the video camera in the air.

"Wait until Naylor sees this! It's just what he wanted! You were both brilliant... although I thought you went a bit too far there for a while, Aisling!" Tosh would have preferred to have sounded cool and detached but he couldn't help letting his jealousy show.

"Ah Tosh! Don't tell me the big green-eyed monster has got to you!" mocked Caroline.

"I just did it to make him feel on edge, Tosh!" explained Aisling.

"He wasn't the only one who was feeling on edge! I wanted to come in here and kick his frigging brains out. Anyway let's lock up here and go and watch this on the video. Me dad's gone for a game of darts in The Bowlers' so we've got plenty of time."

Caroline picked up the tape recorder which she had left over the fireplace. She was worried that Gary might have noticed it so she had asked Aisling to keep him distracted. They both agreed that flirting with him would be the best way of preventing him from spotting both the recorder and the hole in the wall from where Tosh was busy filming. Tosh locked the door as the three of them made there way upstairs to Tosh's flat.

As they came out onto the fifth floor balcony they heard an angry roar from the car park below. It was Gary. He was cursing and swearing out loud.

"Come out, you lousy shower of gobshites! Wait until I get my hands on ye! I'll bloody murder ye!"

"I wonder what's the matter with him?" whispered Aisling. In the early evening darkness they could see nothing out of place in the car park below.

"I think he'd prefer his car with four wheels!" came the husky reply. It was Sledge who had been waiting for them on the balcony. He stood there grinning widely as he waved a four point wheel brace at them. His brother Mattie was there too, giggling like a baboon!

"It was a cinch!" he told them, "We had them off in two minutes!"

"Damn it!" screamed Gary as he kicked the car. He walked out of the Heights leaving the vehicle behind. It was the only car in the car park – and at that precise moment it was possibly the only one in Cork – which was sitting on four rectangular concrete blocks!

Chapter 21

The Lights Go Out

Naylor watched Gary drive away for his appointment with the late Miss O'Farrell at quarter to six. He was standing outside The Slim Jim, a trendy bar and nightclub situated across the road from the equally trendy River Bank luxury apartments. He wasn't sure which apartment belonged to Gary but he knew the block and he guessed that there would be a name alongside each doorbell on the ground floor. He guessed right. Number 31 belonged to P G Ó Coigligh. He had plenty of time. All he had to do now was to get inside the apartment.

Naylor thought it would only be a matter of some minutes before somebody would leave the block and open the main door on the ground floor. He would enter at exactly the same time. Sledge had shown him how to prise the door to Gary's apartment using a chisel. However, he daren't use the chisel on the main door. It was too dangerous. Somebody would surely notice.

After about half an hour he was beginning to despair. There was no sign of anybody. Suddenly he noticed a shadow moving down through the staircase. A young lady came to the main door. This was his chance. He had to make it look as if he was entering as she was leaving. He held the key of his own front door in his hand and moved to put it into the key hole. She opened it first. Yes! At the last second he dropped his own key. Instead of waiting for him to pick it up she simply slammed the door behind her and trotted of into the night leaving him in a crouched position, searching on the doorstep.

"Damn it!" muttered Naylor. "She didn't even wait to see if I found it!"

It was another twenty minutes before the door was opened again. This time it was by a couple who were on their way out for the evening. Naylor waited until the door was actually open before he made his move this time. He slipped inside before they had time to notice him.

"You got there before me!" he told them as he put the key to 42 McGillicuddy Heights back into his pocket.

He was amazed to discover how easy it was to pick the lock with the chisel. Sledge had warned him that Gary might have had a mortise lock fitted which would be impossible to force. Luckily Gary wasn't as security-conscious as he ought to have been. To Naylor's relief he had neither mortiselock nor alarm. He got into the apartment without any damage to the door.

The apartment was neatly furnished with potted plants and futuristic paintings on the walls. Naylor had a good look around for places to hide in case he was disturbed. The computer was in the smaller of the two bedrooms which Gary obviously used as a study.

Naylor sat down and turned it on. Glancing at his watch he realised he had lost valuable time waiting for the front door to be opened. It was quarter to seven. Gary would be on his way home. He would have to move quickly.

Gary was fuming when he saw his car left sitting on four concrete blocks. At the top of the laneway he found his wheels with each tyre deflated. He would have to go home and get the footpump. He normally kept this in the car but he had taken it home to pump up footballs for training the other night. He decided not to ring the gardai. There was little point. They wouldn't be able to do anything about it anyway. There was no real damage done. It wasn't as if the car had been stolen or crashed. Besides he didn't want the gardai asking him what business he had at the Heights. There was no point in rousing suspicion about himself.

He thumbed down a cab on the main road.

"River Bank apartments!" he told the driver.

"Are they the yuppie flats off MacCurtain Street?"

"Apartments!" Gary corrected him abruptly.

"Anything you say... sir!" came the driver's cynical reply.

It had been a strange meeting. He found Miss O'Farrell a

difficult customer and as for her daughter... she was some cookie! Fourteen years of age and the way she flirted with him! However, they were all the same in the end he thought to himself as the taxi drew near to River Bank apartments. They all needed money!

"Thank you, sir! Have a pleasant evening!" smirked the driver as Gary paid him.

"Unlikely!" grunted Gary as he slammed the door and crossed over the road to the apartment block.

Gary knew immediately that he had an unwelcome visitor. Even though Naylor might have thought that he had done a good job with the chisel in gaining entry to the apartment he had made one very basic mistake. He had forgotten to close the door behind him. This was partly due to the fact that he hadn't planed to stay very long and partly because he was petrified.

Gary pushed the door gently and stepped inside. He picked up a baseball bat which he kept in the hallway alongside the coatstand and clenched it. His heart raced as he scanned each door. He carefully turned the handle on the living-room-cum-kitchen door making sure that there was no "'this door needs oil" squeak. Seeing that there was nobody there he moved on to the study. With his ear to the door he was sure he could hear somebody breathing within. He turned the handle just as Naylor put his hand on it from the inside. Naylor reacted more quickly. In a reflex movement he turned the key which had been left in the lock. Gary banged at the door.

"Come out!" he roared.

Naylor made towards the window and opened it. He looked out onto the courtyard three stories below. There was no way he could possibly jump. Fear held him in a sudden tight grip. If he jumped he was dead. If he didn't jump Gary would surely do his best to kill him anyway. The door shook loosely as the hinges began to buckle and bend. Naylor had to make his mind up. He climbed out onto the window ledge as logic yielded to panic in his confused and terrified mind. Suddenly the door burst open. Gary recognised him immediately and charged towards the window-ledge. Naylor froze. Every muscle and sinew in his body gelled into one tight knot as Gary pulled him by the thighs, leaving the upper half of his body dangling precariously on the outside.

"You little sod, Naylor! I should leave you drop!"

"Please, Gary!" pleaded Naylor, whose head was the nearest point to the concrete courtyard thirty feet below!

"Please! I'll give you 'please!' you manky little worm."

Gary let go of Naylor's thighs and left him fall a little further grabbing him again by the ankles at the critical last moment. Naylor, like a drowning man, saw his life pass before him in fleeting split second images. He was afraid to scream in case Gary would panic and drop him. He could feel Gary wrapping one arm around his ankles, holding them in a half nelson, while he searched through his pockets with his free hand.

"Please Gary! Let me up! Pull me in please! Please!"

Then with all the strength still left in his lungs he began to scream hysterically. Gary realised he was in danger of attracting unnecessary notice from the neighbours. He quickly hauled him in and left him flop to the carpeted floor like a sack of potatoes.

Naylor looked up. He could see a blurred image of Gary hovering over him holding a piece of paper which he couldn't distinguish. Maybe hanging upside down for so long had caused a sudden rush of blood to the head resulting in loss of vision. He tried to focus but the image remained blurred and the piece of paper still indistinct. He put his hand to his head to straighten his spectacles and suddenly realised the reason for the blurring. His glasses were gone. They had probably fallen down into the courtyard as Gary had held him out to dry.

Suddenly Naylor felt vicious kicks coming at him rapidly as Gary exploded in a fit of violent rage! He curled into a hedgehog-like ball in an effort to protect his face and stomach. Each kick caused him to wince with pain and grew with intensity as Gary's anger reached fever pitch.

"So you know about me, Naylor!" he bellowed.

"No Gary! I don't! I know nothing! I didn't know this was your place! I just broke in to look for money!" Naylor lied pathetically. "I'm a crack addict! I do these places all the time!"

"You lying toe-rag!"

Gary pulled him up by the hair then started bashing his head against the leg of a wrought iron bedpost. Blood spurted out from different wounds on his forehead as Naylor heard himself screaming for mercy. When the screaming grew hysterical Gary threw Naylor onto the bed and stuffed a tea towel into his mouth which he tied with a wire flex. Then he started pounding him with punches. Naylor could scream no more. A wave of nausea washed through him. He could feel the impact of the punches but not the pain anymore. He had gone beyond pain. In a strange way he felt victory was his. No matter how hard Gary tried he could no longer hurt him. His body was numb and immune to the punishment it was receiving. If he had had the energy left he would have loved to have laughed out loud. A wild and victorious laugh. Then as suddenly as it had started the beating stopped.

There was more tying up. This time both his hands and feet were yanked up behind his body and tied with what felt like an aerial lead. He was told to lie face down on the bed and not to move. Then he heard some drilling and banging as Gary was obviously rehanging the door of the study.

There was more silence before the door slammed closed and the key was turned. Then there was darkness as the lights were switched off and Gary left. Naylor felt his heartbeat ease then rise again as he swam against the waves of a nauseous tide until his own lights went out.

Chapter 22

Coming To

When Naylor came to he was fully aware of where he was and what had happened to him. This pleased him. Even though every bone, muscle, tendon and tissue in his body ached, his mind was still alert. He listened for signs of life in the apartment. There were none. Apart from the traffic of the busy city streets outside he could hear nothing. He wasn't sure of the time or for how long he had been out cold. He knew it was still night-time as the room was pitch black. But whether it was the darkness of early evening, dead of night or pre-dawn, he wasn't sure.

He knew it was important to keep his mind working and not to drift back into a state of unconsciousness. He began to think of his mother whom he hadn't seen since Tuesday night, the night before the game in Dublin. She had improved a lot since the operation. Physically she had made great progress. Her broken bones were mending nicely. Mentally however he wasn't so sure. She was very restless. She shuffled in the bed any time anything was said to her. She smoked incessantly swallowing the smoke deeply as she inhaled. This upset Naylor as she had given up smoking for Lent two years ago and had sworn that she would never go back on them.

She refused to tell the gardai anything other than a transparent yarn. She told them she was followed home from the shops by a man whom she didn't recognise. She came in and locked the door. Next thing she knew he forced his way into the flat, beat her up and turned the place over. All he had taken was some jewellry, ten pounds and some loose change. She said nothing about her missing social security and children's allowance books. Naylor knew why. She didn't want the gardai to think that it was the work of a shark. She was frightened that had she told the gardai anything it would be worse for her the next time.

Naylor could get no more information from her other than what she had told the guards. He knew that she was lying. She knew that he knew that she was lying. In the end they didn't talk about the attack at all.

"The less you know about it the better, Tony. You'll be safer that way!" was her final comment on the affair. Little did she know how accurate she was being at the time.

Naylor had seen his mother's books in a pile which Gary kept in a drawer of the study desk. Naylor read through them all recognising several names of women who lived in the Heights. He fingered through the pile and found himself thinking of the agony that these women must be daily enduring. Held to ransom by the local baker.

That's how he was caught. As Naylor read the names of Gary's victims and thought about their plight, he didn't realise that time had run out. He should have been on his way back to the Heights. When he felt Gary's hand on the other side of the door handle he realised he had blown it.

He tried to undo the knot which was keeping his hands tied to his feet but it was too tight. Gary must have been one hell of a boy scout he thought. He could certainly pack a punch too! Why did he go berserk like that? Naylor couldn't understand. One minute he decides to have mercy on him and not let him free fall to his death and the next he is beating him to a pulp. Naylor remembered the blurred image of Gary reading something before the assault. The questionnaire! That was it! That's what he was reading before he started his kick-boxing routine! He had written Gary's code number and other information about the computer network on the back of it!

So Gary now knew that Naylor was not only suspicious but had the ammunition to put him away. He knew that Naylor had found out about McGuinness Finance. What would he do next? Naylor knew what he had to do. He had to get bloody well out of that apartment!

He guessed that by constantly wriggling he would prevent cramps and the dreaded pins and needles. He had to keep his circulation moving. Already, by moving his jaws as vigorously as he could, he had loosened the tea towel which was gagging him. He discovered that by coughing and retching the towel was further loosened. Gradually, as he contorted his facial muscles, he felt the flex which had secured the gag slipping from the back of his head to his neck. Soon he was able to spit out the tea towel completely. The sudden rush of air to his mouth made him feel light-headed yet exhilarated. One down one to go. As he began to twist his wrists and ankles he suddenly heard voices as the front door of the apartment opened.

"Just stay with him until I get back! He's locked in the study! Don't attempt to go near him!"

"Are you going to call the guards?"

"I don't know yet. I know the lad's mother. I wouldn't like to upset her. I'm just going to call around to her now and explain how I found him here rooting through my stuff. Anyway I've got to collect my car. It's over in the Heights. Some joker left the air out of the tyres. I'm going around there now with a foot pump."

"Is that what you have in the bag?"

"Not that it's any of your business, but yes it is!"

They spoke in hushed tones which Naylor could barely make out. He realised that Gary had no intentions of going near the guards. He had obviously brought around a couple of heavies to keep an eye on him.

"Remember, don't go near the study. It's locked and it's to stay locked!"

"Sounds a bit like kidnapping to me! I don't like the sound of this, Mr Quigley!"

"I think he's right, Mr Quigley. Kidnapping is a serious thing."

"Is that what you think is it?"

"Yeah!"

"Listen you stupid little good-for-nothing! I pay you to do as you're told not to bloody well think! Now do you want to make twenty quid or not!"

" ...I suppose so... "

There was something familiar about that voice thought Naylor as he struggled to hear what was being said.

"Well, sit in the kitchen there, have a couple of beers and I'll be back to bring the little twerp home to his mother in an hour!"

The door slammed. Naylor waited for a minute or two before he let out an elated roar.

"Eureka! Geronimo! Open the door and let me out!"

Naylor had recognised the identity of his two reluctant babysitters yet Hulk and Ringo weren't too sure about him.

"Who's in there?" asked Hulk cautiously.

"It's me, Naylor, Tony O'Neill from the Heights... I'm a friend of Sledge's!" Naylor never thought he'd see the day when he'd say that.

The door was forced open for the second time that evening as both Ringo and Hulk rammed it with their shoulders.

"God in heaven! What happened to you?" asked Ringo in astonishment when he saw Naylor tied up in a bloodstained heap on the bed.

"Just get me out of this!" Naylor muttered through his swollen lips.

Chapter 23
Under Arrest

Ann Marie McGuinness didn't usually work late on Thursdays but since she had spent most of Wednesday at the match she decided to do some catching up. When Ciarán and the others left the offices of McGuinness Finance at half past five, she settled down at her desk and buried herself in paperwork.

She had heard the buzz of an incoming message on her computer, but didn't bother to turn to read it immediately. This wasn't unusual. Agents often faxed or sent computer messages in the evening so as to have them on her desk by first thing the following morning. It wasn't necessary to leap to attention every time the familiar buzz sounded. However this particular message buzzed a while longer than usual and aroused her curiosity. She turned to read the screen. Her eyes widened as she sat back in disbelief.

MISS MCGUINNESS
MY NAME IS TONY O'NEILL.
I WAS IN YOUR OFFICE YESTERDAY POSING AS A STUDENT ON A COMPUTER ASSIGNMENT.
THIS WAS UNTRUE. I WAS INVESTIGATING THE ACTIVITIES OF P G Ó COIGLIGH, OR GARY QUIGLEY AS HE PREFERS TO BE CALLED IN CORK.
HE IS A FRAUDSTER. HE USES YOUR COMPANY AS A FRONT FOR HIS OWN MONEY-LENDING OPERATION.
IN SHORT, HE IS A SHARK. WE HAVE VIDEO EVIDENCE OF HIM IN ACTION. I INTEND GIVING THIS EVIDENCE TO THE GARDAI IN CORK TONIGHT. I FELT YOU SHOULD KNOW IN ADVANCE.
I'M SORRY TO BREAK THE NEWS TO YOU THIS

WAY. I HAVE TO GO NOW AS I'M IN HIS APARTMENT. HE IS A VERY VIOLENT MAN. I KNOW THIS BECAUSE HE HAD MY MOTHER BEATEN UP FOR FAILING TO MEET A REPAYMENT. SHE'S A CLIENT OF YOURS. MRS BETTY O'NEILL, 42 MCGILLICUDDY HEIGHTS, CORK, REF: CK/34526/PG. HER DETAILS ARE ON YOUR SYSTEM. CHECK HER OUT. HER ACCOUNT IS OFFICIALLY PAID UP. IT'S A PITY THAT GARY DIDN'T THINK SO.

She didn't know how to react. This could have been one of Pádraig's pranks but she knew it wasn't. It just wasn't funny. Suddenly lots of things began to make sense. She had been very impressed by the three students the previous day in the office but she did feel it was rather strange that they should pick her relatively small operation for their school project. Usually they would go to big factories or banks. Ciarán had left the three of them alone in the office for quite a while. They could easily have got the information they needed in that space of time.

She typed in the reference number of Betty O'Neill and saw as Naylor had seen the previous day that the account was paid.

She thought of Pádraig or was it Gary. She had only known him for a few weeks when he began to pester her for part-time work. He kept telling her how badly the bakery was going and how he really wanted to sell up and get out of it. He was very charming. Always sending her flowers and ringing her late at night. When her Cork agent asked for assistance she couldn't think of anybody better or at least more eager. However, since she gave him the position, the late night phone calls had become less frequent and the sending of flowers had stopped altogether.

He had only come up on Wednesday because she had phoned him and told him that a client had given her two complimentary tickets for the match. No this was no prank.

This Tony O'Neill had done her a great favour. Nobody tries to pull one over on Ann Marie McGuinness MD. Right, Mr Quigley, I'll fix you, she thought as she reached for the phone and punched each number angrily.

"Could I speak to somebody in the Fraud Squad please... I wish to report a serious crime... Yes of course... I'll hold... "

At nine-thirty Tosh could stand the waiting no longer. Naylor had said quite clearly that he would meet them back at the flat at eight. Gary had left at half past six, so even if he had to walk to his apartment he would have been there before quarter-past seven.

"If he called a cab he would have been there even sooner!" he told Aisling who was also beginning to worry. Caroline had gone home ages ago leaving the two of them alone in the flat.

"Come on, Tosh! Let's get the bikes and go over to those River Bank apartments. Naylor might be in trouble."

"You're right, Aisling!"

"Will we bring the tapes with us and drop them in to the Garda Station on the way?"

"Naylor wanted to do that himself but at this stage I think we should go ahead and bring in the guards ourselves. Sure we have enough on these to have Gary locked up for years!"

On their way down to the basement shed they looked into the car park to see whether Gary had returned for his car. Down below they could see a figure frantically trying to steady a wheel back on to its axis.

"It's him!" whispered Aisling.

"He must have gone home to get a pump or a jack! I hope he didn't bump into Naylor!" replied Tosh as the two knelt down behind a pillar on the third floor balcony.

Suddenly a squad car zoomed into the car park with a siren blaring and its blue light flashing. Two uniformed gardai climbed out followed by two detectives.

"Naylor must have contacted the gardai himself!" whispered Tosh.

"Ssh... I want to hear what they're saying!" said Aisling.

Gary stood by his car holding a wheel brace.

"Having a spot of car trouble, sir?" asked one detective cynically.

The other detective walked up to him and took the wheel brace from him calmly. She looked Gary straight between the eyes.

"We've been watching you for the past half an hour putting those tyres on. We were going to move in sooner but I said to myself 'why not let him put the tyres on first then we'll have our little chat'. You see otherwise one of my uniformed friends here would have had to put them back on and they are messy old things tyres aren't they sir?" Gary looked timidly at his oil smudged hands. "Now about our little chat," continued the detective. "My name is Detective Inspector Maeve Scully this is Detective Pat Casey. And your name is...?

"Quigley... Gary Quigley."

"Yes I know Gary... or is it Pádraig?"

"Gary... Gary will do fine!"

"Will it? Oh I am pleased about that. It's so much easier to arrest somebody who tells us his real name."

Suddenly her voice changed from its soft cynical tone to one which was officious. As she spoke the other Detective, Pat Casey, winked at the one of the uniformed gardai who grabbed Gary, turned him around and handcuffed him.

"Gary Quigley, I am arresting you on suspicion of the attempted murder of Mrs Betty O'Neill... "

The words rang musically in the ears of Tosh and Aisling who hugged with delight as Gary was led to the squad car. They ran down the three flights of stairs and into the car park.

"Excuse me!" roared Tosh. "I think this might come in handy!"

One of the uniformed gardai turned around. It was Linda. The garda who had been so kind to Naylor the night his mother had been beaten up.

"Tosh, isn't it?" she asked, remembering his face.

"Yes, Linda, and this is Aisling. We have Quigley on video."

Tosh told her the story of how they lured Gary into Miss O'Farrell's flat and fooled him into offering Caroline, alias Miss O'Farrell, a loan.

"That was a very foolhardy thing to do. You might have got yourselves badly injured," she said as she took the tapes from Tosh.

"It was Naylor's idea!"

"You mean Tony?"

"Yeah Tony... We always call him Naylor... Was it he who phoned you?"

"Er, not exactly. We actually called on him. He's in hospital!"

Naylor lay contentedly on the flat of his back. He had one arm in plaster and and a bandage covered three stitched wounds on his head. He had spent the last three hours undergoing intensive medical examinations. Luckily, his injuries, although extensive, were not too serious. However, the doctors wanted him to stay in hospital for a few days as a precaution. They also promised to fix him up with a new pair of glasses!

He would have loved to have seen the look on Gary's face when the gardai arrived into the car park. As soon as Hulk and Ringo had untied him the gardai arrived. They immediately phoned an ambulance. He wanted to go to the Heights with them first but they wouldn't hear of it.

Despite his pain he lay there with a smile as wide as Cork Harbour. He sipped a Seven Up through a straw as he lay propped up on four fluffy pillows. He closed his eyes and sighed with satisfaction as the words "Yes, I did it!" echoed in his mind.

Outside there was a queue of people waiting to talk to him. The garda wanted a statement. They had brought along a photographer and a forensic specialist to file a report on his injuries.

Tosh was like an expectant father pacing up and down the waiting room. He had always felt responsible for Naylor. Whenever Naylor had got himself into a fight in the yard at primary school Tosh would inevitably come to the rescue. But earlier that night, while Naylor was being beaten to a pulp by Gary, where was he? He was at home, marvelling at his camerman skills as he watched the video over and over again with Aisling. God, he felt like such a jerk.

Aisling sat there twiddling her thumbs anxiously praying that her friend was out of danger. Ger Twomey sat next to her cursing himself over and over again.

"My God! What kind of a legal guardian am I. My first day officially on the job and the poor kid ends up in hospital while I'm over in The Bowlers' thinking I'm Eric Bristow! I wouldn't mind but I didn't hit the bloody board all night!"

"It's not your fault, Dad. We should have told you."

"Damn right you should have told me! There's no way poor old Naylor would be in there now fighting for his life if you'd have let me in on your little plan!"

"I know, Dad... "

Tosh wanted to apologise further but he was stopped in his tracks as a nurse wheeled Betty O'Neill in to see her son. She didn't seem to notice any of them. She looked very feeble and distressed. She had her head down and appeared to be crying as the nurse whispered words of encouragement.

Naylor sat up cheerfully when he saw his mother. He put his pain on hold as he hugged her with his free arm and kissed her cheek.

"Oh Tony, love! What have you been up to?" Tears flowed freely down her face as Naylor told her his story. She sat back and listened with pride, as he recalled the events of the past two weeks through aching jaws and throbbing lips.

"Oh Tony!" she said through her tears when he had finished."What would I ever do without you?"

"It's okay, Mam," whispered her son as she buried her face in his lap. The pressures of the past few months seemed to swell and erupt at that moment as she sobbed bitterly. Tony fought back his own tears as he comforted her. He stroked her greying hair and started rocking her gently as he told her repeatedly in a Rock-A-Bye-Baby tone, "It's okay, Mam... It's okay... It's all over now."

Chapter 24
The Final

St Johns, or "The Heights" as they were more commonly known, lined out for the final of the Under Fourteen football final under a new manager. Ger Twomey was delighted to be offered the position. He rose to his new task with an enthusiasm he hadn't experienced since his own playing days when he too donned the green and gold of St Johns. His pre-match pep talk had his team convinced that they were unbeatable. He made each of them feel as if all they had to do was to step on to the pitch and walk away with the cup.

The atmosphere at the stadium was electric. It was the first time any of them had ever played in Pairc Uí Chaoimh and the prospect of getting ready in real dressing rooms and walking out through the tunnel onto the famous turf of "The Park" held them all in awe. Even the substitutes, who were normally disgruntled at not making the first fifteen, relished the thought of sitting on the bench in a real dugout. When Ger Twomey finished his rousing pre-match pep talk, they were all raring to spring into action on this the biggest day of their playing careers to date.

Tosh, however, was the exception. It's not that he wasn't excited at the idea of playing in "The Park". It had always been a dream of his to play on the same pitch as his heroes on the Cork senior team. Neither had he a problem with his dad being in charge of the team. Far from it. As most of the team came from the Heights and the surrounding area nobody knew the players better than his father. He had watched them all growing up. This season alone he had been to all the home games and had often walked long distances to see the away matches. With a week to go to the final against Bishopstown, Ger Twomey was the obvious choice as a replacement for Gary who was currently a guest of the Minister for Justice, on remand in Cork Prison.

No, it wasn't anything to do with his father that had Tosh's mind straying from the task in hand of beating Bishopstown.

Aisling had told him the news the day before. They had a half day from school due to a staff meeting and Aisling wanted to go to the park. There was something she wanted to tell him. Something important.

They sat on the same bench near the swings. There was an uncomfortable silence between them. Aisling was reluctant to tell him straight out. Tosh could sense that there was some bad news heading in his immediate direction. They began to engage in small talk, mostly about Naylor, his mother and Saturday's final. The small talk fizzled out slowly and was followed by another long silence. Tosh grew impatient. Aisling stared straight ahead at the ducks who had swam to the side of the pond in the expectation of some left over crusts. Tosh was worried. Why won't she look at me? He feared the worst. The look on Aisling's face suggested only one thing. After a while he could stand the silence no longer.

"Aisling?"

"Yes?" she still stared straight ahead.

"Is there something you wanted to tell me?"

She nodded but kept her eyes away from his.

"Let me guess... you don't want to go out with me any more?" said Tosh

"No," she replied without looking in his direction.

Tosh was confused. "Is that no, you don't want to go out with me anymore, or no, I guessed wrong and you do want to go out with me?"

"It doesn't matter what I want, Tosh," she told him as she turned to face him for the first time.

"What do you mean by that?"

"I'm going to live in France," she announced.

"Oh?" Even though Tosh's response barely amounted to a grunt in less than one syllable, it didn't hide his disappointment.

"Mum thinks it would be a good idea if Dad and she tried to make a fresh start."

"So why doesn't she just come home?" suggested Tosh hopefully, as he began to see Aisling's face disappearing from his future vision of life.

"Well, that's what I was hoping," Aisling told him. "I kept telling her every time she phoned that Dad had really improved and that he was genuinely missing her. I begged her to come home and give him a chance. I heard him telling her the same thing too. I know we had her convinced, so much so that when she phoned last night I expected her to say that she was phoning from Cork Airport. She spent over an hour talking to Dad. She spoke to me then and told me that herself and Dad had decided to try again. She wants him to invest his redundancy money in my grandmother's restaurant in Bordeaux. Dad jumped at the suggestion. He reckons it will be a great opportunity for them to work together. So that's it, Tosh."

"I suppose."

More silence...

"When are you leaving?"

"Next Sunday."

Tosh's heart sank. "That soon!"

There was a long pause as they both looked away from each other and pretended to renew their interest in the crumb-searching ducks.

"Well, that's bloody marvellous!" explained Tosh as he flung a whole cheese sandwich into the pond sending the ducks into a frenzy.

"I'm sorry, Tosh. I don't want to go to France," she told him.

"Me neither... I mean I don't want you to go to France either," said Tosh as he foresaw some lonely months ahead. He stood up and threw the rest of his lunch into the pond to the delight of the ducks who cackled their approval.

"Come on!" she told him rising to her feet. "You can walk me home."

"I'll call around on Sunday with the bikes," he told her as they stood outside her front door. "I'd bring them tomorrow only we have the final. Will you be there?"

"I don't think so... I have a lot to do. Packing and... "

Her voice trailed off. She stared him straight between the eyes and moved closer towards him. Suddenly she put her arms around his neck and her lips on his. She kissed him. It was a long, deep lingering kiss. Tosh thought he was going into orbit. For the past three weeks he had been looking for a way to make this happen and then it happens without his even having to try. His mind floated lightly causing him to feel giddy. Here was the girl he had always wanted to kiss, kissing him. He expected any moment to wake up! The words, "Is this really happening to me?" danced repeatedly in his mind as Aisling's mouth circled his deliciously. Then, as suddenly as it started, it stopped. Aisling smiled, told him she'd see him on Sunday, wished him good luck in the final and closed the front door behind her.

When Tosh played well the Heights usually won. On the rare occasion that he was playing below form then his team didn't have a prayer. Unfortunately for the Heights it seemed as if Tosh had waited for today to play at his worst. Every ball he jumped for, he missed. His first twenty minutes was a litany of errors. Bishopstown maximised on the Heights' misfortunes and led by nine points as half-time neared.

"Come on, Tosh!" roared Naylor from the sideline. "Get into the bloody game!" He had been discharged from hospital the day before and was back living in the flat with Tosh and his dad. He had intended to watch the game from the covered stand with the rest of the Heights' contingent but ended up joining the substitutes and selectors as guest of honour in the dugout. The past week had been great. His mother had picked up tremendously and couldn't wait to be discharged. She had even cut down on the cigarettes and promised Naylor that she would give them up altogether once she came home.

Naylor couldn't believe his eyes. At first he thought it might have been his new glasses! No sooner had shouted his last piece of advice to Tosh when his friend mis-timed another handpass. The ball fell directly into the arms of his opposite number. Another point for Bishopstown, courtesy of the absentminded Tosh and Bishopstown take a ten point lead.

Tosh couldn't stop thinking of Aisling. He had a good look around at the crowd before the game but he couldn't spot her. He listened to every shout from the crowd hoping to hear her voice. Every time the ball went to the side of the field he found himself scanning the spectators for her smile. He was playing dreadfully. Once or twice he saw his father burying his head in his hands after he had fumbled a ball and sent another shot wide. He had to settle down. He had to try to concentrate. But how? All he could think of was her smiling face, her lips on his and that sweet taste of roses. The whistle sounded for half-time. Thank God for that, he thought, and he wasn't alone!

In the dressing-room at half-time Tosh knew he was in for a roasting. Bishopstown were ten points ahead and had the benefit of a strong breeze in the second half.

"And that's where we'll get them!" roared Ger Twomey enthusiastically. "They think that just because they have the wind behind them they can't lose that lead! But we'll turn this game around on its head in the second half! We'll show them!"

He didn't mean a word of it! As far as Ger Twomey was concerned the cup was on its way to Bishopstown but he had to try and sound confident. After all he was the manager!

"Now, Tosh, for God sake get a hold of yourself, son! Just relax! You're too bloody edgy! Keep your eye on the ball and your mind on the game. And how about a solo run from ya?"

Tosh knew his father was right. He was behaving like a moron. This game meant so much to the people from the Heights. Five double-decker busloads of them had come to see the game today and he was letting them all down. He had to put Aisling out of his mind and get out on that pitch and do the business.

"So come on, lads!" Ger was imparting his final piece of advice. "One almighty effort! Let's get out there and do it! Come on the Heights!"

The dressing-room door opened and the teams spilled out into the tunnel as they raced out to the pitch. The crowd looked sparse in the huge stand but the noise was deafening as the the Heights supporters roared their encouragement.

Just as he was leaving the tunnel for the pitch Tosh saw her waving at him. Even though he couldn't hear what she was saying it didn't matter. He knew she had come to see him. Aisling had come to see him play! The effect was instant. It was as if the brain cells which governed his common sense suddenly clicked into action. A voice in his head seemed to come from nowhere and whisper "Come on, butthead! Get your act together fast!" Tosh knew that for the next thirty minutes he had a battle on his hands.

The second half was different as Tosh stamped his authority on the game. He scored a point immediately after the restart and followed it with a delightful sideline ball which sailed between the posts cutting the deficit to eight points. The sound of "Come on The Heights!" rattled rhythmically as St Johns kept pressing forward and Bishopstown saw their first half lead being whittled away. Suddenly Tosh found himself on the halfway line after catching a high ball cleanly. While his marker was still looking for him, Tosh took off on a solo run.

"That's my boy!" roared Ger on the line, who subconsciously slipped out of the role of manager and into that of proud father.

"Go for it, Tosh! Go for it!" Naylor had jumped off the bench and was waving his arms including the plaster-clad one in the air. He was playing the role of proud best friend!

Tosh neared the goal. He was about twenty metres out. A point would have been a safer option but he saw Nipper McCarthy screaming for the ball, unmarked and to his right. This time the handpass was perfectly placed and Nipper had no problem slipping the ball past the hapless Bishopstown keeper.

The stadium erupted! Aisling hugged her father whom she had persuaded to come along to see the game. Naylor raced up and down the sideline punching the air and yelling, "Here we go! Here we go! Here we go!"

From then on it was only a matter of time before St Johns, The Heights, took over the game. Sledge was at the back of the stand leading the chanting. On the field the players were spurred on by the ongoing vocal support. With only seconds remaining the teams were level.

Tosh was exhausted. He had never run as hard in any game. He rose to field another high ball and again took it down cleanly. He was away from his marker. He raced towards the goal with what seemed like the entire fifteen Bishopstown players pulling and dragging from his shirt. Again he saw Nipper screaming inside him for the ball. He had to choose. Pass to Nipper. Try his own shot. He tipped the ball to Nipper who was immediately jumped on by the Bishopstown players who had been climbing all over Tosh. The referee blew his whistle without hesitation. Free kick.

Tosh was forty metres from the goalposts and facing into a strong wind. The referee informed him that he would have to score directly as this was the last kick of the game. Tosh inhaled deeply. His legs wobbled like jelly. He was thoroughly drained. The crowd hushed to a virtual silence as he placed the ball. He took four paces back and took one more deep breath. This was it. This one was for the Heights!

The ball soared high defying the resisting wind. The delicious echo of leather on leather accompanied its flight as it continued to rise before it dropped between the posts and over the bar. He did it! St Johns, The Heights, were the champions!

Chapter 25

Finally

School on Monday was an anticlimax after the celebrations of Saturday night. Tosh wasn't saying very much. Naylor fully understood so he didn't bother trying to cheer him up. This was his first day missing Aisling. It couldn't have been easy. It wasn't as if she had gone to Mars though. She would be back in a year or so. Still, he decided to leave Tosh alone. He wasn't ready for advice just yet. He would wait until lunchtime.

"You can write to her, can't you, Tosh?" he asked him in the canteen when Tosh's silence began to irritate him.

"Shut up, Naylor!" grunted Tosh as he munched a Toffee Crisp slowly.

"I'm just trying to make you see that she won't be in France forever and that you can still keep in touch in the meantime." Naylor had put on his favourite hurt voice. It worked. Tosh felt guilty for snapping at him.

"Yeah, you're right, Naylor. I could write every week or two."

"Of course you could. Knowing you, you'll probably write a book each time. Heh! You could write her one of your poems!"

"What poems?"

"The ones you keep under your bed that you don't want anybody to see!"

"You read them!" barked Tosh angrily.

"Yeah! Your dad and myself had a look through them one day that you were meeting Aisling!"

"You what?" Tosh pretended to be furious.

"They weren't bad, Tosh! But listen, I've got to go. There's someone I must have a word with. I'll see you back in class."

Tosh watched as Naylor got up and sat next to Pauline who was sitting alone at an adjoining table. He had met her on Saturday night at the the Heights' victory disco in the community centre. Aisling had brought her along as Pauline was dying to chat up Naylor! She had put all other boyfriends on hold. Naylor was a bit of a hero in the school at the moment. The story of his tracking down Gary had made headlines in the local paper. Suddenly Pauline found Naylor very interesting. Naylor was likewise beginning to change his opinion of Pauline.

"Three weeks ago you said she was the greatest snob in Ireland! What's made you change your mind?" Tosh asked him after the disco.

"But do you know, Tosh, she's really a very nice person once you get to know her. She has a lovely personality!" he explained unconvincingly.

Tosh cleared the table where he had been sitting and headed back to class. Biology was next. He usually sat with Aisling for biology. The excitement of the weekend was all but a memory now. He sighed as he entered the laboratory and took out his books. Naylor was right. He could keep in touch by writing. But was it worth it? He was only fourteen. Was he too young to have such feelings? Maybe it would be better to try and forget about Aisling and get with on with things. After all she might meet some French guy and forget about him altogether. He'd feel a proper twit then if he was sending her weekly letters!

Miss Jameson, the biology teacher entered and immediately began to rattle on about flowers, pollination, stamens, filaments and anthers. She was going to give out flowers for them to dissect and analyse. Tosh was reminded of roses. The delicious smell of roses. He took a clean piece of paper from his pad and began to write...

55 McGillicuddy Heights,

Dear Aisling...

Watch out for some other great books from
BLACKWATER PRESS

The Cally

by Turlough McKevitt

Following a walk on Slieve Gullion, a strange creature stalks John Kett. Curious things begin to happen. Rex the dog mews, the Ketts fly and Mary Kett almost jumps out of a giant nut!

Granny clashes with Olivia Jolson, the famous theatrical director, during the staging of the pageant to celebrate the finding of the "Gretel Stones".

Meanwhile... events draw them all towards the Mountains of the Hag, where they are eagerly awaited by... **THE CALLY.**

The Yuckee Prince

by Larry O'Loughlin

When Witch Wendy Way is asked to babysit Prince Alysious Tripod Jefficus, she can't believe her luck. After all, it has only been two days since she left the Grimwood Academy for the Training of Wizards and Witches.

But she soon finds out that *luck* isn't always *good* luck, when the sweet little prince with the face of an angel lives up to his well-deserved nickname of ***"The Yuckee Prince"***.

Ignatius The Wonderful Pig

by Patrick O'Sullivan

Ignatius MacTaggle is no ordinary pig. Noble and refined, yet lovable too, he lives in the lap of luxury in Ballymactaggle Hall. But when his master dies his whole world is turned upside down. With his new-found friends, Lucy and Gavin, he sets about making his master's dream of helping old unwanted donkeys a reality. But first they must contend with the scheming plans of Peregrine, the new owner of the Hall, and Lucy's arch rival, Rachel.

Can Ignatius and Lucy outwit their enemies, or will Peregrine and Rachel have the last laugh?